THE ISLAND SCANDAL

Getaway Bay, Book 2

ELANA JOHNSON

ISBN-13: 978-1638760047

Chapter One

B urke Lawson parked his truck outside the main building at Petals and Leis, his family's flower farm in the hills. After getting out, he drew in a deep breath of the fresh, perfumed, morning air, glad he'd beaten the sun to work this morning. As usual.

Burke rarely slept past four, and he didn't care if his early bedtime contradicted the persona he had to maintain. Somehow, the knowledge that he hadn't been on a second date—or even a real first date—in years got around to the right people.

And that was how he liked it.

His father pulled into the lot a few minutes later, dressed for business like normal. He'd taught Burke everything he knew about the fields, the land, the flowers. Not to mention the fertilizers, the harvesting, the reseeding. And that was just the growing side of things.

Burke had to know about sales too, and management,

and hiring. He spent time in the shipping department to learn how to keep flowers fresh, how the deliveries worked, all of it.

After all, when his dad was ready to retire, Burke wanted to be ready to take over the business, keep it in the family, preserve what generations of Lawsons had built.

"Morning, Dad," he said, drawing his father's attention to the bench Burke liked to sit on in the morning as the sun rose over Hawaii and painted Getaway Bay in gorgeous, golden light.

His father took a few moments to find him among the foliage, and Burke lifted his hand and grinned.

"What are you doing, hiding there?"

"Dad, I sit here every morning while I wait for you to show up." Burke stood and stretched as if he'd been out partying all night.

His dad wore an expression that expressed his disappointment at such a prospect and dug in his pocket for the keys to the building. Burke had a set too, but he liked to wait for his dad, this morning ritual of theirs something he didn't want to give up yet.

"How's Mom?" he asked.

"Doing a bit better." His dad unlocked the door and stood back so Burke could enter first. He took a long look at his dad as he passed, finding that his blond hair had started to turn white. When had that happened?

Burke ran his hands through his own flop of light, sandy-colored hair and threw a smile at his dad.

"You look tired," he said. "You getting enough sleep?"

"Yeah, Dad, when I can." Burke didn't tell him that the insomnia plagued him every night, no matter how much melatonin he took or how long he meditated.

"Stay out too late?"

Burke inhaled to deny it, but instead, he let the comment slide. That way, he didn't have to admit that he spent every night with Dolly, his golden retriever who had a slobbering problem.

He walked side-by-side with his dad into the office space, but Burke bypassed his and settled in the chair across from his dad's desk.

He'd put his keys in the top drawer, and wake up his computer. He'd read a few things, and they'd be out in the fields and orchards in thirty minutes or less.

Burke let his father go through the motions, somehow finding peace in them. Something had been seething inside him for a while now, and he hadn't been able to name it.

But it wasn't peaceful or soothing. He felt…unsettled. But he had no idea how to cure himself.

"Ready?" His dad stood and reached for the sun hat hanging on the hook beside his desk.

Burke stood too, glad the routine this morning had taken less than fifteen minutes. He yearned to be outside, away from walls, where he wouldn't feel so caged. He collected a baseball cap from the top of the bookcase in his office and followed his father outside.

"Let's go out to the plumeria orchards." His father grabbed a set of keys from the drawer in the desk by the back door, and Burke braced himself for a hard conversation. His dad only went out to the plumeria orchards to say something that had been bothering him for a while. Burke supposed he should be grateful for his dad's predictability, but his heart felt like a hunk of lead in his chest. He really didn't want to have to defend himself today.

It was almost comical that his dad couldn't see through Burke's carefully constructed reputation. But not many could.

Ash can, he thought as he climbed into the passenger seat of the side-by-side recreation vehicle they used to get around the huge flower farm. With over a dozen varieties of flowers being grown on the property, Petals and Leis employed over sixty people year-round and required seven-days-a-week attention.

Today, as they maneuvered along the dirt road between two fields, Burke caught sight of at least half a dozen people already at work among a field of bright pink carnations.

As the engine kept him and his father flying toward the trees on the far edge of the property, Burke considered coming clean about what his life was really like. But then he'd have to delve into why, and he didn't think he was ready to open that door quite yet.

Once again, the thought of his best friend, Ashley Fox, popped into his mind. She'd recently come out of a relationship with a guy she'd thought would propose. Six months later, and Burke could still see the heartbreak on her face whenever he asked her about it.

His failed relationship was six *years* old, but he thought he'd done a decent job of hiding his feelings from everyone. After all, everyone loved a good sense of humor, and he could keep the party alive with a few well-told jokes and a single well-placed smile.

Even Ash had never questioned him much about Bridgette.

His father parked the ATV and got out, a sigh leaking from his lips as the gray sky started to lighten with shades of yellow and gold. Burke pushed his hand through his hair, thinking it was probably time to get it cut, and positioned the hat low over his eyes.

If his father wanted to talk, Burke needed some sort of barrier.

His dad wouldn't say much for the first few minutes anyway. If he did, it would be about the trees, the flowers, or their business.

Sure enough, as he moved into the trees, pushing toward the larger, more mature grove at the back, he said, "Petals and Leis has been very lucky to stay in the family for so long."

"Mm," Burke said noncommittally. He'd heard this before. Six generations of the family-owned business was no joke among the Lawson's.

"It's almost your turn," his dad said.

"Yeah," Burke agreed. "I want the farm, Dad. You know that, right?"

"Of course." His father trailed his fingers along the trunk of a plumeria tree that stood about fifteen feet tall. In mid-summer, the trees were practically dripping with blooms, but Burke somehow knew he and his father weren't there to harvest. In fact, he thought he remembered seeing the plumeria harvest on the schedule for next Monday.

"The plumeria are my favorite flowers," his dad said. "So beautiful. So serene."

Burke loved them too, only because on the many hikes he'd taken around Getaway Bay and the other Hawaiian islands, every time he looked up, he only saw greenery. But here, looking up through the trees brought an explosion of colors that made his soul sing with happiness.

"Burke, I'm almost ready to retire," his dad said, turning back to him. "I want to pass the farm to you."

Burke sensed a *but*, and he paused too. His muscles cinched like someone had pulled a drawstring on them. Tight. Tighter.

"You need a haircut," his dad said, a frown in the words that was mirrored on his face.

"I can get a haircut," Burke said.

"You need to settle down," his father said next, his gaze even and the frown gone. "Your mother and I love you, but we want this farm to stay in the Lawson family for six more generations."

Burke blinked at his father, unsure of the meaning of the words. "I want that too, Dad."

His father's head cocked to the side. "Do you?"

"Of course I do."

"So…who do you think you'll pass the farm to?"

"I—" Burke's voice died, sudden understanding stealing the life from the words and the air from his lungs.

He wasn't married.

Wasn't even dating anyone.

Didn't want to date anyone.

Or get married.

"The twins like working here." His dad turned and started walking again, more of a stroll than anything else. They certainly weren't working this morning. "But neither Kayla nor Krista wants to run the place."

"*I* want to run the place," Burke said, the thought of not having his morning ritual of coming to this land choking him. "I've lived for this place for twenty-five years, Dad. I love this land, and these flowers, and I want to take over when you retire." He caught up to his father, strength and bravery coursing through him now.

He put his hand on his father's arm and got him to stop. "Dad, what are you saying? That I can't have Petals and Leis because I don't have a wife? A—a kid?"

Desperation raced across his father's face. There, then gone. He squared his shoulders and said, "We'd like to see you settle down before I retire. We'd feel more comfortable if you had even a girlfriend. Someone you were even remotely serious with."

Burke felt like someone had punched him in the throat and then the stomach. So many things churned inside, and he had no idea how to respond.

Sadness passed over his father's weathered face now, and he shrugged. "I'm not saying you can't have Petals and—"

"I have a girlfriend," Burke blurted, silencing his father and causing his eyebrows to fly sky high.

"You do?"

"Sure," Burke said, turning away so the little fib couldn't be discovered so easily.

"Who is it?"

"Ash." Burke said the first person that came into his mind.

"Ashley Fox?" The level of disbelief in his father's voice soared toward the heavens, and it would be a miracle if Ash didn't hear it all the way down the hill at her cute little beach cottage.

"Yeah," Burke said. "We've been friends for a long time, and I don't know." He shrugged. "Started seeing each other a few months ago." He pressed his eyes closed, needing to talk to Ash, stat. They were scheduled to run in another hour, and he'd have to figure out how to get her to play along with this ruse.

"Well, great," his dad said. "You should bring her to the company barbecue in a couple of weeks."

"Yeah, sure." He felt like he'd swallowed a whole bag of jumping beans, and now they were pinging around inside his stomach, screaming things like *This is a bad idea!*

You need to call her right now!

There's no way you can pull this off!

Ash will never agree to this.

He tried to silence them, but they stuck with him for the rest of the hour, and when he showed up at the beach to meet Ash, he barely knew his own name.

Burke managed to stretch, his calves protesting at the long hold until he finally stood. Ash was late, and that only increased Burke's anxiety.

Dolly barked from near the shoreline, and Burke turned toward the golden retriever. The sun glinting off the bay blinded him, but he thought he saw a woman jogging toward him.

Finally. He could talk to Ash and they could make a plan.

He couldn't lose Petals and Leis. Not over something like this. He'd buy himself some time with Ash, and then he'd figure out how to move past Bridgette and find a real girlfriend.

He had to.

"Ash," he called as he started toward her. But Dolly whimpered and darted right at him, bashing into his shins before Burke could avoid the canine.

He grunted and found himself sprawling toward the sand. A moment later, the grittiness of sand filled his mouth and stung his eyes and squished between his fingers. Pain flared in his legs and back, and his whole face felt aflame with embarrassment.

"Burke?" Ash arrived with a mouthful of giggles and

bent over him. "Really graceful," she said, offering him her hand to help him stand.

He gazed up at her, realizing in that moment how pretty she was haloed by the early morning light. Since her break up just before Christmas last year, she'd let her hair grow out, and only the bottom few inches were still bleached and silvery.

She sobered the longer he stared at her. "You okay?" She sat back on her heels. "What's with Dolly?" She glanced over her shoulder toward the water while Burke got control of his emotions—and his hormones.

This was Ash. Ashley Fox. A girl he'd known since he was fifteen years old and she was thirteen. His running partner for the last decade.

Not his girlfriend, no matter what he'd told his father only an hour ago.

Burke pushed himself up and started brushing the sand off his body. "I don't know, but I have something to ask you."

Chapter Two

Ashley felt something brewing in the beachy air, but it wasn't a storm. Burke continued brushing sand from his shirt, a look of distaste on his handsome face.

He's not handsome, Ash told herself. So she'd been fighting a crush on her best friend for sixty-three days. It wasn't a crime, and Burke would never know.

He sighed in the most exasperated way and reached back with one hand and pulled his shirt right over his head. "I have sand everywhere." He shook the blue T-shirt while Ash stared at his tan, broad shoulders and then pushed her eyes toward the sky.

Every cell inside her body burst into flames, and she needed to run. Now. "I'll go check on Dolly."

"No." His hand shot out and grabbed her wrist. "Wait."

She looked into his ocean blue eyes and let herself dive in for a moment. Just a moment. That was all she gave herself each day. A moment to imagine what holding his hand would be like. A moment to think about asking him to her niece's birthday party so she wouldn't have to go alone. A moment to consider stopping by his house after she checked on her mother each evening.

And she'd already had her moment when she found him handsome and ogled his beach-running body.

"Wait?" She pulled her hand out of his fingers. "You're acting weird today. Everything okay?"

He stared at her for another moment, shook his shirt again, and pulled it back on. "I'm fine. Let's run." Burke started down the beach, whistling through his teeth for his dog to come with. Dolly did, apparently whatever had startled her no longer an issue.

Ash started after him, but his pace was blistering, and she didn't catch up to him until he reached the top curve in the bay. Even then, her chest felt like it was her first day of running instead of a habit she'd picked up fifteen years ago after her first year in college had added twenty pounds to her petite frame.

Once Burke had found out about her morning ritual, he'd asked to join her. It hadn't been a problem. In fact, he pushed her to work harder, run faster, like she was now.

"Did you get bad news or something?" she panted as she matched her stride to his. He had six inches on her easily, and his legs seemed to eat up more sand with one step than she got in two.

"I'm fine," he said again, which totally meant he

wasn't. After his last real girlfriend broke up with him five or six years ago, Burke had run like this. Like he could get away from whatever was plaguing him by running up and around the east bay and then Getaway Bay.

Ash really hoped they weren't going that far today. It was their fifth day running this week, and she'd planned a three-miler.

"Well, I have some news," she said, determined to babble to herself if she had to. She didn't like running in silence, and she'd given up headphones and music years ago. Burke was usually a chatterbox during their morning runs too.

"Yeah?"

A one word answer was better than *I'm fine*, so Ash employed her bravery to tell him what she hadn't told anyone. She often used him as a sounding board, but she'd moved forward without him this time.

"Yeah, remember how I said I was bored with my life? That I needed a change?"

Burke came to a sudden and screeching halt, sand actually spewing forward as he stalled. His chest heaved and sweat ran down the side of his face and dripped from his jaw. "You need a change." He wasn't asking a question, and Ash saw that storm she'd felt earlier, swirling right there in his eyes.

"Yeah," she said, wiping her forehead and wishing she had a hair appointment for later that day. As it was, she had a wedding dress to finish, and chicken teriyaki to make, and a mother to go visit. "Remember I said that?"

She sucked at the air, ready to be done with this weird morning of running.

"You're bored with all the wedding dress sewing."

Bored wasn't the right word. Ash had known since the time she was thirteen that she would sit behind a sewing machine for a living. The first time she'd experienced that needle zipping along, in and out, in and out, creating something beautiful from flat fabric, she knew.

Burke drew her attention away from the glinting water undulating out in the bay. "Ash?"

"Yeah?"

He hesitated, and then asked, "What's the news?"

"I signed up for scuba diving lessons." The very thought of being underwater terrified her. Maybe another reason she'd always known she wouldn't leave Getaway Bay. Sure, she could dip her toes in, swim in a pool, or even wade out until the water reached her waist.

But she did not like going underwater.

"Wow." Burke's breathing started to steady, but he looked as red as a boiled lobster. "You don't even swim."

"I know how," Ash said, rolling her eyes. She'd expected more support from Burke. But he was looking at her like she'd lost her mind. Maybe she had.

"When is this happening?"

"I just need a *change*," she said, the desperation coating the last word. She didn't even try to hide it, not from Burke. She looked at him, willing him to understand.

"I'll go with you," he said in that best friend voice

she'd grown to love over the years. "When's your first lesson?"

"Tomorrow morning."

He blew his breath out. "I can make that work."

Ash nudged him, a playful open palm to his shoulder. "Maybe you should consult your calendar, Mister Party Animal." She added a laugh, mostly to cover up the zing racing up her arm and into her shoulder.

"Come on," he said, turning away.

"What?" Ash sidestepped, and only seeing half of his face was enough to see the clench in his jaw.

"You know I'm not a party animal." He spoke quietly, almost like he didn't want the waves to overhear. No one else was out on the beach quite yet, though she expected to see the Thompson twins at any moment.

"Yeah, I know." She stepped beside him and mirrored him as they faced the water.

"I have nothing on my calendar tomorrow morning, except work at Petals and Leis."

"So you can come?"

His hand fumbled down her arm and into hers. Ash sucked in a breath as he said, "Of course."

Maybe he hadn't heard her. But this hand-holding was so brand new, and Ash felt like a party paraded through her whole body.

"Burke, what's wrong?" she asked, her voice a bit on the high-pitched side.

"I have to tell you something, and I want you to let me finish before you say anything."

Ash swallowed and nodded. He'd only asked her to wait until the end of what he had to say once before. And that was when he'd given a little speech about leaving the island for a while to get a second degree, this one in accounting.

She'd missed him terribly during those few years, and he'd come back a different man than the one she'd known when he'd left. He was a little livelier, a lot more guarded, and the only one she trusted with everything.

Well, maybe not her crush on him.

Because Burke Lawson didn't date, at least not for real. Not since he'd come back to Getaway Bay. And he'd never looked at her with anything but playful friendship in his eyes.

Just like he'd never held her hand.

She pulled away and said, "Go on, then."

"I need a favor." He ran his hands through his flop of blond hair, and Ash wished she could copy him.

"Anything," she said.

Hope lit up his whole face. "Really?"

"Sure," she said. "We're best friends, Burke. If I can help you, I will."

Why he didn't smile, she wasn't sure.

"I did something stupid." He swallowed.

"It's okay," she said.

"I told my dad—okay, well, my dad said he's almost ready to retire. I want the farm. He wants to give me the farm. But he and my mom want me to settle down first."

Ash waited, thinking his parents had a reasonable

request, though no one worked harder than Burke. He could run Petals and Leis without any problems. But she also knew it was a family company, and that fact mattered a great deal to his dad. To Burke too.

"So are you going to give up your fake reputation?" she asked.

"Yes." Another swallow. "That's where you come in."

"Me?"

"Yeah. I told my dad we were dating." He put both hands on her shoulders and peered down at her, desperation in his wide eyes. "Will you be my girlfriend? Just for a few weeks."

The air left Ash's lungs, and she just stared at Burke. Was he serious? Had he learned of her crush somehow? Had she been too obvious?

She didn't know, and she couldn't answer. So she just kept staring.

Chapter Three

"Maybe a month," Burke heard himself say. He felt like he was floating outside of his body, and Ash didn't seem to be breathing or blinking at all.

She tipped her face toward the sky and started laughing.

Burke frowned, his hands dropping to his sides. This was no time to laugh. They needed a *plan*, immediately. He couldn't believe he'd allowed himself to run a mile before telling her.

"Breathe," he said, wondering what was so horrific about being his girlfriend for a few weeks.

Ash took in a deep breath and reached out her hand like she needed something to hold onto. He grabbed her and steadied her. "Breathe, Ash."

She did, and he noticed as her freckles popped out on her skin until she got more color in her face. "I was not expecting that."

Burke wanted to ask what she was expecting, but he figured it was along the lines of attending a scuba diving lesson with him. Or, in his case, holding his phone while she recorded him trying to catch a big wave during one of his surfing sessions.

"My dad is serious about this." Burke let go of her hand and paced away for a few steps. He turned back and returned. "He wants the flower farm to stay in the family for six more generations. I want that too. I do." He exhaled, glanced at Ash, who still hadn't moved, and paced away again.

I just don't want to date, he thought.

But that wasn't it. The real cause of the unsettled feeling in his gut—which had been there for six long years—was the fact that he didn't want to risk his heart again. Didn't want to get hurt again. Didn't want to fall in love with a pretty woman only to have her tell him she wasn't that serious about him.

An experimentation that didn't work out.

Pain lanced through his chest all over again, and he flinched. When he faced Ash again, she'd squared her slight shoulders. "All right," she said. "I said I'd do it, and I'll do it."

"Really?"

"On one condition."

Burke's hopes stalled in the way they rose. "A condition?"

"I need to know your plan for finding a real girlfriend."

Of course Ash would ask for the hardest thing of all. Burke had always been able to tell her the truth. Well, about most things. Not Bridgette. And not how her older brother had warned him not to fall in love with Ash.

Burke had laughed at that, as he'd never looked at Ash with any idea of kissing her. But as he studied her now, he saw her beauty and imagined himself sweeping his hand along the side of her face and into her hair just before he kissed her.

After all, a boyfriend had to kiss his girlfriend, right?

There were so many details to work out, and Burke couldn't order them all, especially not with the fantasy of kissing Ash in his mind now.

"Burke? Tell me you have a plan for finding a real girlfriend."

"I don't have a plan for that," he said, pulling himself back to the present. Any kissing that happened would be an act. "See how badly I need your help?"

Ash rolled her eyes, the zombie-like state she'd fallen into gone now. "You realize this is two favors, right?"

"What can I say?" Burke said. "Our friendship has always been easy. This is just a slight complication." He grinned at her, and she narrowed her eyes.

"Are you seriously giving me your flirty smile right now?" She slapped his chest, causing him to fall back a step in the sand. "You realize that only works on women who think you're cute."

He put his hand over the spot she'd hit. "I prefer handsome."

She shook her head, her ponytail swinging from side to side, but she wore a smile that said she'd still go along with this.

"This is never going to work," she said.

"Oh, come on." He slid his arm around her shoulders and started back down the beach toward their meeting spot. She lived in a cottage near there, and he whistled for Dolly to come along.

"Remember that play you were in in tenth grade? You *slayed* that."

She scoffed out half a laugh. "I was terrible in that role, and I never got cast in a play again."

"Yeah, but—"

"And no one says slayed anymore." She elbowed him slightly in the ribs, and he recoiled like she'd really hurt him.

"So I'll come by tonight, and we'll make a plan?" he asked.

To Ash's great credit, she said, "Yeah, all right," before continuing down the beach and disappearing between a couple of trees on her way to her almost-beachside cottage.

Burke stayed on the beach for a few more minutes, mostly to calm his still accelerated pulse.

Ash really was his best friend.

They could do this.

And so what if he'd enjoyed holding her hand? That didn't mean anything.

Did it?

Burke had no idea, and he had so many other problems to solve, he couldn't add another thing for his mind to riddle through.

———

HIS PHONE SNAPPED, CRACKLED, AND POPPED AS HE entered his office that evening. He'd spent the morning in the fields and then the afternoon in the accounting department, as they were gearing up for an annual conference and would be out of the office for a week just after the company barbecue.

He didn't have to look at his phone to know it was Ash. He'd set that notification specifically for her, because of her love for the crispy rice cereal that made the same noise. In fact, Ash could eat cereal for every meal—and she claimed to sometimes do just that.

Burke didn't really believe her. Number one, he knew she was a diva for a hot lunch. She got cranky if she couldn't have one, and said a peanut butter and jelly sandwich or a salad simply wasn't good enough.

He also knew she cooked every night for her mother, who was slowly getting worse and worse as her cancer progressed. After her father had died about five years ago, Ash had taken on the evening routine of checking on her mother. Her older brother, Leo, went sometimes, but he had a demanding job and two young kids.

Burke couldn't believe he and Leo were the same age. They'd been best friends all growing up, and still were despite apparent differences in their lives. Of the two Fox's, Burke preferred Ash these days, as Leo had never approved of Burke's friendship with his little sister.

And once he found out about this relationship?

Burke sighed as he removed his phone from his back pocket to check Ash's message. Leo would probably come knock Burke's door right off its hinges and demand to know what he was thinking.

I have a ton of leftover lobster fritters, Ash had texted. Just bring the sodas.

Burke smiled at the message. If there was a better food on the planet than Ash's lobster fritters, he didn't want to know. She served them with two sauces: a lemon mayonnaise or a sweet honey glaze. Burke sometimes dipped his in both sauces, which made Ash wrinkle that cute little nose of hers.

He dropped his phone when his fingers spasmed. The resulting clunk! echoed through the empty office. "Cute?"

Burke's face heated though he was alone. When had he started thinking Ash was cute? "Maybe about the time you started holding her hand," he muttered to himself as he bent to pick up his phone.

Luckily, the screen hadn't cracked and he hurried to thumb off a response about the fritters. He didn't need to ask what kind of soda she wanted. She only got one thing —the pretty in pink—from Maui's. He wasn't sure why she liked pink grapefruit, raspberry, and cherry in her Diet Coke, but he didn't have to drink the stuff.

He left the office, swung by the soda shop, and arrived at Ash's cottage in time to see her walk through the front door and close it behind her. For some reason, he stayed behind the wheel of his sports car and watched that blue rectangle for a moment.

They'd painted it together, about a year ago. She'd told him about her first date with Milo, and Burke had made fun of the man's name. "Sounds like a cat," he'd said, and Ash had swept blue paint up his arm and laughed.

Milo had turned out to be just as nasty and stand-offish as most felines, and he certainly didn't like Ash's friendship with Burke. She still ran with him every morning though, and they just didn't talk about Milo— until he broke up with her.

His phone snapped and crackled, and Ash had sent, I'm thirsty. Come inside already.

Burke smiled at his phone, collected the sodas, and walked across her grass. Most people in Hawaii who lived a few feet from the beach didn't worry too much about grass. But not Ash. She mowed it and watered it and put fertilizer down in the spring. Her grass was one of her most prized possessions, and Burke gave it a grin too.

He went in without knocking and said, "Your pretty in pink," before brandishing the tall soda cup toward her.

"Why were you just sitting out there?"

"Thinking," he said.

She sucked on her straw for several long seconds. "Mm, this is so good." She smacked her lips as Burke noticed the black skirt she wore. It fell to her knees and hugged her curves. She'd paired it with a yellow blouse with white stripes, and she was classy and chic and cute all rolled into one package.

"How's Deb?" he asked, his tone only slightly strangled. He wasn't sure why his thoughts had chosen today to betray him, but he was determined to stay until he and Ash had a reasonable plan for their fake relationship.

"She's actually doing okay," she said. "Claims to not like lobster anymore, but, okay." Ash shrugged and turned back to the kitchen. "That's why I have so many leftover fritters."

"I'm always up for a lobster fritter." Burke wondered when the conversation would turn toward his insane request from that morning, and he decided as he watched Ash start to unwrap the lobster fritters and set out the sauces that he'd just let her dictate the pace of the conversation. He usually did, and they'd always gotten along so well because of it.

"Just one?" she asked, a teasing glint in her eye.

"All of them." He grinned as he sat at her bar and let her get them on a tray and into the oven to crisp up again.

She turned toward him and exhaled. "So. What's the plan?"

"Plan?" Burke echoed. "That's why I'm here tonight. We're going to make the plan."

Displeasure sat in her dark eyes. "Tell me you have some idea of how and when we started dating."

Burke brightened. "Sure, yeah. I told my dad we'd been friends for a while and decided to try, I don't know, something more a few months ago."

"A few months." She folded her arms.

"Yeah." Burke watched her, realizing he'd already messed up. *Of course you did—the moment you opened your mouth and told Dad you had a girlfriend.* "Bad?"

"I think it should be a few weeks. You're not that great at time stuff, so it'll be fine."

"Why a few weeks instead of months?" Burke asked.

Every shutter Ash possessed flew into place, and she turned away from him. In the past, Best Friend Burke would've let her shut herself off and they would've moved on. Eaten. Talked about nothing. And he'd have gone home without worrying about why she'd shut down.

But now…something itched, clawed, craved to know what was going on inside her head. Why it should be weeks instead of months. Why Ash had that adorable blush in her cheeks.

"Ash?" he pressed, something he hadn't done much.

She turned back to him, her eyes storming, and said, "Because, Burke, I've only been broken up with Milo for a few months," in a tone that indicated he should've known that.

Chapter Four

Ash bent to get the fritters out of the oven. They'd had plenty of time to heat, and she could escape to her bedroom to change while Burke ate.

"I'm sorry, Ash," he said, real quiet. The real Burke, the one he hid from everyone but her had arrived. Finally. "I didn't know about Milo. I mean, obviously, I did, but yeah. I am bad with time and dates."

She set the tray of fritters on the stovetop and turned toward him again. "It's fine. I'm going to go change. You eat. And then we'll figure things out." She walked away, her heels making clicking sounds on the kitchen tile until she stepped onto the carpet.

In her bedroom, with the door closed and locked, she sank onto her bed and kicked her heels off with a long sigh. She wasn't sure they *could* figure things out.

"Maybe if you weren't attracted to him for real," she whispered, glad she didn't even have a pet to overhear her. If his request had come sixty-four days ago, or sixty-five, she'd be fine. She'd laugh and shake her head and start thinking of all the single women she knew she could set him up with.

But now?

Now she wanted to be his girlfriend, and she'd have to pretend she didn't want to be while she pretended to be....

Her head hurt. Nothing made sense, especially while wearing a tight pencil skirt and a blouse that had a tag that had been scratching the back of her neck all day. She changed into her softest T-shirt and a pair of gray leggings, another sigh escaping now that was more about comfort than confusion.

She returned to the kitchen, stalling for a moment—her third moment that day—to admire Burke's wide shoulders as he sat at her counter and ate her fritters.

"Good?" she asked, continuing into the kitchen to sit beside him.

"*So* good," he said, putting the last bite of a mayonnaise-covered fritter in his mouth.

"Okay," Ash said, reaching for the notebook she kept on the counter. "What color do we want our agreement in? Pink? Green? Or purple?" She grabbed all three pens from the mug next to where her landline used to be.

"Don't you just have black?"

"Purple, I think. This feels like it should be in purple." She flipped open the notebook and wrote at the top "Agreement between Burke Lawson and Ashley Fox."

She had no idea what to write next, so she looked at Burke.

Those eyes, so full of wonder and life and as blue as the day was long, sucked her in and she let herself fall. A sigh may have even come out of her mouth.

"You're serious about this," he said.

She yanked herself back to reality. And the reality was, she and Burke were not dating. "Don't you think we should be?" She sat up a little straighter and resisted the urge to doodle something in the corner of this very official document. "I mean, there might be kissing and stuff."

Her mouth turned dry at the very prospect of kissing Burke.

He gaped at her. "Kissing?"

She gave him her best dirty look, but it didn't even faze him. It usually didn't. "Burke. I realize you haven't had a real girlfriend for a while, but if we want this to be convincing to *your father*, kissing is definitely a possibility."

His gaze turned heated, and Ash had a hard time from melting into him. "Definitely a possibility. Maybe we should start practicing now." He lifted his eyebrows, that playful twinkle in his eyes maddening and swoonworthy at the same time.

She elbowed him and said, "Nice try," in a very convincing tone. But if he could see the way her heart was dancing around her chest, he'd know she wanted to kiss him right now.

"So what goes on this?" she asked.

"I have no idea," he said. "I didn't think we'd do a whole contract thing."

"It's not a contract. It's an agreement."

"Can you come to the Petals barbecue in a few weeks? Can't we just hold hands and act like we're falling madly in love with each other? Does that have to be spelled out in an agreement?"

"Let me get my calendar." She heaved a great sigh as she got off the barstool, like Burke was this huge burden she simply couldn't carry for much longer. But holding his hand sounded wonderful. And she wouldn't be acting like she was falling for him.

"You know, most people have moved out of the stone age," he called after her. She didn't flinch, look back, or respond. A few seconds later, she returned to the kitchen, her paper planner in her hand.

She spread it on the counter between them. "When's the barbecue?"

"July third."

"I have a wedding on the second," Ash mused. "And the Getaway Bay parade is that morning." She glanced at Burke, not allowing herself to truly settle her eyes on him before looking back at her paper planner. "Fireworks the next night though."

"We can do it all," he said. "Parade in the morning. Barbecue that afternoon. Fireworks the next night."

Ash didn't dare hope to spend that much time with Burke. Sure, they saw each other often—running on the beach alone was an hour everyday. They sometimes met up at night, especially if Burke wanted to perpetuate his party animal reputation. He'd make a brief appearance somewhere, then slip off into the night, wander down the beach to her cottage, and sleep on her couch.

But this was a different kind of time. This would be family time. Company time.

Girlfriend time.

Ash wrote the events in her planner in pencil. She'd learned long ago that even the most solid of plans could change. "What about between now and then?" she asked. "Are we keeping this relationship secret, or....?"

"Well, it seems like we've been doing that for a few weeks," he said, reaching for the last lobster fritter. "Right?"

"Oh, so we're ready to make the relationship public."

"Yeah, I think so. I mean, now that my parents know."

All at once, Ash sucked in a breath. "Oh, my mom." She moaned out the last two words. "Burke, I can't—she can't—if she thinks I'm really dating someone seriously enough to meet his family, she'll start to see white dresses and silver bells everywhere."

Panic flowed through her with the strength of a tsunami, and she did look fully at Burke this time. His face was blank, though, which didn't comfort her at all.

"She doesn't leave the house much, does she?" he asked.

"No, but Leo goes over there a lot, and she has friends who come visit. She'll find out." She pushed the notebook away and dropped the pencil over her planner. "I don't know, Burke."

He finished his fritter and got up to wash his hands. With him on the opposite side of the counter, Ash could think a bit clearer. Did he know his cologne called to her? It was like it was specifically engineered to make her pulse pound and her cheeks heat.

"Maybe we should go talk to your mom tomorrow," he said, weight and caution in each word. "Tell her we're dating, and it's casual for now, and you'll keep her up to speed with everything."

"My mother is a bloodhound," Ash said. "Have you forgotten she taught kindergarten for thirty-two years? She knows a lie from down the hall and around the corner."

Burke pressed both palms into the counter like he needed the support to keep standing. "What do you want to do, Ash?"

When he spoke her name with that much compassion, the emotion real and raw, she wanted to confess everything to him. But she held her tongue. This wasn't the first insane crush she'd had on the man, and it probably wouldn't be the last.

Well, unless he got married. Or she did.

She shook her head. No, she wasn't even looking for a date, not after Milo had taken her heart and skipped across the ocean to Cancun.

"I don't know," she said.

"So you don't have a plan for everything."

She jerked her attention to him and found that charming smile on his face, those eyes practically dancing with mischief. "I don't have a plan when my best friend wants me to pretend to be his girlfriend."

Burke's smile faltered. "What are we going to tell Leo?"

Ash cocked her head, trying to find more in what Burke had asked. "What does he have to do with any of it?"

"Nothing, I guess." But Burke turned away from her and started cleaning up the tray where she'd warmed the lobster fritters. She let him drop the subject, though she wanted to urge him to share more details.

She'd tried before, and Burke was particularly tight-lipped when he had to be.

"Let me feel out my mom," Ash said. "Okay?"

"I'll follow whatever you want me to, Ash."

She nodded and closed her planner, their evening clearly concluded. But Burke didn't leave, and Ash sat next to him on her living room couch while he flipped through her channels. She had a scuba diving lesson in the morning, and when she reminded him about it, he grinned from ear to ear.

"I'll go then," he said. "You'll probably want to stare at the ceiling and fret for a while before you fall asleep."

"I will not." She practically shoved him toward the front door. "Now get out."

He laughed as he stumbled out onto her porch, and she closed the door behind him, quickly darting to the living room window to watch him saunter over to his black, sporty car. He got behind the wheel, cast her house one last look—which caused her to duck below the windowsill—and drove away.

Ash indeed did lie in bed and stare at the ceiling for a while. A long while. But it wasn't the following morning's scuba dive that had her stomach in knots and her heart skipping beats.

It was Burke.

He'd never looked back to her house like that, like he had more to say but didn't know how. With such seriousness in the set of his strong mouth. With such indecision in his eyes.

"Indecision," she told the plaster. That was what she'd seen. But what did it mean?

Chapter Five

B urke held two cups of coffee, hoping that stopping for the brew was a boyfriendly thing to do. He'd never brought Ash coffee before, but he'd done all kinds of things for Bridgette. If she mentioned a salad in a text, he showed up at her office with it for lunch.

When she'd said she loved poodles, he'd bought one and trained it to ring the doorbell before giving it to her. That had taken months, and she'd given the dog to a friend when she'd left the island.

Not back to Burke.

His throat burned with acid, and he took another swallow of his own coffee to get it to go away. But it had never really gone away. He didn't understand women like Bridgette, but he'd been hopelessly in love with her. How he'd missed that she'd been using him for a solid year felt like a stab through the heart every time he thought about it.

So he didn't think about it.

"Is that for me?" Ash's voice cut through the breeze coming off the water and the self-loathing thoughts in Burke's head.

"Sure is." He smiled up at her like they had paparazzi watching their every move, trying to catch them in the lie of their fake relationship. "Double vanilla, whip."

"Medium roast?" She took the coffee and lifted the cup to her nose. "You got it, Burke." She smiled at him, which sent a strange vibration through his chest, and sat beside him on the boardwalk. "Thanks."

Burke didn't answer. He was still trying to figure out if he'd just experienced a thrill when his best friend had said his name, or maybe he had a heart murmur and should go see a cardiologist as soon as her lesson concluded.

"Hold my hand," she hissed, and Burke's pulse leapt like he'd been shocked.

"What?"

"One of the girls—forget it." She slipped her hand into his, and this time Burke had no doubt as to why his skin felt tingly and his chest tightened. He couldn't believe it, but he really liked holding hands with Ash.

Why had he never done it before?

Leo bounced around his brain while Ash stood and made a high-pitched introduction of "Burke Lawson, my boyfriend," to a woman named Riley. Apparently she worked at Your Tidal Forever, the wedding planning joint that gave Ash most of her wedding dress business.

The two women talked while Ash kept a vice grip on his fingers with one hand and lifted her coffee to sip in the other. Burke paid attention. He knew he'd have to remember Riley's name and get on her good side if he wanted a chance with Ash.

Then he shook himself as he realized what he'd just thought.

But did he want a chance with Ash?

Was this really pretend?

She sank back to the boardwalk after Riley had left, her shoulders slumping. "Oh my heck. Do you think she believed me?"

"Yeah, sure," Burke said with an air of nonchalance. But he didn't know Riley and had no way of telling what the woman believed or didn't believe. "There's your instructor."

Ash groaned. "Maybe I should reschedule. I'm tired."

"Staring at the ceiling?" He glanced at her and squeezed her hand, which was still securely in his though no one was around to perform for.

"Yes, if you must know." She lifted their joined hands and shook his. "Because of this." Then she exploded to her feet, tossed her remaining coffee in the nearby trash can, and practically stomped through the sand toward the scuba diving instructor at the water's edge.

Burke looked at his hand. "Because of this?" He got

up and followed her, much slower and with dozens of questions filling his mind.

"Hey, man."

He looked up a few steps before he was about to collide with Ryan Bonnett, the scuba instructor.

"Oh, hey." Burke let the huge, muscular man do a hand slap and shake, though he'd never liked the guy much in high school and even less now that he was a buff scuba god parading around the beach in tiny swimwear.

Ryan's dad owned a yacht club, and he'd grown up in the water. He obviously operated the scuba diving lessons as a branch of the club, as everything in sight said Bonnett Yacht Club on it in swirling gold letters.

Suddenly the sun was too hot, and he didn't want to wait around in it while Ash had her lesson with this guy.

"You ready, Ash?" Ryan asked.

"It's just you two?" Burke looked back and forth between Ash and the very handsome—and still single—Ryan.

"Yes," Ash said, answering both questions. "I paid for a private lesson. Well, a series of them." She pinged her gaze between Ryan and Burke too. "He's just here for moral support."

Ryan looked at Burke with an expression that said *That's cute*, and proceeded to instruct Ash in how to wear the wet suit, and the tanks, and all the readings on them. Burke frowned through the whole thing, wondering if Ryan had to stand that close to Ash while he showed her the dial. Wondering if that touch along her waist lingered just a little too long.

Ash didn't seem to notice or care, and she turned back and waved at him as they approached the dock. Burke put a smile on his face and threw his hand in the air, but as soon as she turned around, the glare and frown returned.

He watched them get on the boat—just the two of them—and start out toward the pinnacle of the bay. He had nothing to do but wait, so he went to the end of the dock where their boat had been and sat down, his legs dangling over the water.

In that moment, he realized he was jealous. Jealous of Ryan Bonnett, because he didn't want Ash to fall madly in love with the meathead and sail off on some yacht.

"It's just a scuba lesson," he told himself for a solid hour until their boat returned.

Ash's peal of laughter didn't bring him any joy, and as she tossed her wet curls over her shoulder, Burke saw her. Really saw her.

And he liked her for more than his best friend.

He stood and stuck his hands in his pockets, completely out of his element. Off his game. He didn't even know what planet he'd been blasted to.

He hadn't felt this way about a woman in six years, and he'd fully expected never to feel this energy, this attraction, again.

But there it was, coiling in his stomach, ready to strike.

Ash started talking about what she'd done, and the things she'd seen. Burke listened, asked questions in all the right places, and sent her off to change in the yacht club dressing room.

"What's her story?" Ryan asked as he climbed back on the boat to do whatever needed to do whatever needed to be done.

"What do you mean?" Burke asked.

"I mean, do you think she'd go out with me if I asked her?" He cast a long look toward Ash's retreating form. "She's gorgeous. No fear out there."

"Really?" Burke could not imagine Ash falling backward over the side of the boat and swimming beneath the surface of the water. "She's terrified of the ocean, you know. Her dad died at sea."

Ryan picked up a rope and started coiling it as if Burke hadn't spoken. "I like her."

Burke didn't need to get in a match of wits or good looks. Ryan would definitely win anyway. So he simply said, "We're dating," and walked away. He could wait for Ash at her car as easily as on the dock.

"No way," Ryan called after him. "Really?"

Burke didn't turn back and defend himself. But the fact that Ryan Bonnett didn't even believe that he and Ash were dating was definitely concerning.

When Ash showed up at her car, her hair still damp

and twice as curly as it was when it was dry, Burke said, "That guy was going to ask you out."

"Who?"

"Ryan Bonnett, the scuba guy." Burke gestured back toward the general direction of the bay. "I told him we were dating." He glanced around like their relationship was a covert military operation and they couldn't be caught talking about it in broad daylight. "And he didn't believe me."

Ash's eyes widened, and she fished in her purse for a pair of sunglasses. "What are we going to do? If we can't even convince him, how are we going to convince your parents?"

"I don't want him to do your private lessons anymore," Burke said, avoiding her question. He'd been asking it for ten minutes while he waited for her, and he was no closer to an answer than before.

Ash looked up, abandoning the search through her bag. "What? Why not?"

"You're *my* girlfriend," Burke said, maybe a little too vehemently.

Ash blinked like he'd flicked water in her face. Before she could say anything and so he wouldn't have to explain the unexplainable, he said, "Come on, let's just go."

"You drove yourself, didn't you?" she asked.

"Yeah, but." He held out his palm so she'd drop her keys in his hand. "We need to talk. I'll drive. Let's go to lunch."

"It's too early for lunch."

Burke's patience for being on this beach waned. "Fine. Brunch." He clenched his jaw and looked over her shoulder, and she finally got the hint. She pulled her keys from the side pocket on her purse and dropped them into his hand.

He closed his fingers around them, letting the sharp edges of the metal dig into his skin, and walked around to the driver's seat. Maybe if he drove long enough, with the window down and the wind blowing in, his thoughts and feelings would align and he'd be able to face Ash without wanting to kiss her and truly claim her as his.

Maybe.

Chapter Six

A sh let Burke drive away from the beach and down the curvy roads toward the more commercial part of town. He didn't say anything, and Ash didn't like the way the silence felt like it had a life of its own.

He pulled into a seafood restaurant that served lobster and shrimp fritters with sugary glazes, as well as the best assortment of coffees and teas the island had to offer. Ash wasn't sorry they'd come here; she simply had no idea what to say to him as they waited in line, ordered, and then retreated to the patio so she could sip her second cup of coffee of the day.

This one was far superior to the one Burke had brought her in a to-go cup before her lesson, but that was to be expected at Sea Party. She and Burke certainly weren't the only couple at the outdoor tables, but for the first time, she realized that she and Burke looked like they were dating.

That's good, she told herself and it gave her the bravery to reach across the table and touch Burke's hand. "It's going to be okay," she said. "Why does Ryan Bonnett matter?" She looked at him, letting a little bit of her emotion leak into her voice. "I like you. You like me. We can do this."

"It's a different kind of like, Ash." He picked up another fritter and dunked it in lemon frosting.

"Is it?" She hid half her face behind her coffee cup and watched the breeze play with the leaves of the trees.

Their eyes met, and Ash wasn't sure what he could see in hers. In his, she found an edge there she hadn't seen before. Maybe she had, a long time ago. She found worry. She found a slip of hope.

She curled her fingers around his and smiled. "I like you."

He squeezed her hand. "And I like you." And while Ash knew he meant he liked her as his best friend, in that moment, it felt like she might actually be able to have a real romantic relationship with him.

"All right then." She slipped her fingers away. "So we forget about Ryan Bonnett—who I will not be going out with, by the way."

"No?" The playful quirkiness of Burke returned. "You don't like him? You didn't seem to mind when he was inching into your personal space with the oxygen tank."

Ash flinched as she reached for one of the last fritters. "What does that mean?"

"He was a little handsy."

"I didn't notice." She opted for the vanilla glaze, not wanting to tell him that she'd been so nervous about going out on a boat and then flinging herself backward into deep water that she hadn't noticed a whole lot of anything.

But she had to do something about her boring life. She'd spoken true when she'd said she needed a change, and she knew she'd been in a rut since the death of her father.

"How was the boat?" he asked. "For real?"

Ash didn't want to keep things bottled up, not from Burke. Maybe their relationship wasn't real to him, but Ash made a quick decision to pretend it was. Because for her, it felt like a dream come true.

"It was terrifying." She put the last of her fritter in her mouth and looked at him.

Compassion filled his eyes and he reached over and patted her hand. "I'm sure it was."

Ash wanted to shrug and say it was no big deal. That she'd get over it. But she didn't want to get over her father's death. She didn't mind missing him, and she didn't mind helping her mother most days.

She just didn't want to get in the ocean, as it was unpredictable and unrelenting. Perhaps if she knew what had happened to her father's boat that day, she wouldn't be left with so much anxiety about getting on a watercraft and sailing out into the beautiful water most people loved.

But since she didn't know what had happened, she assumed anything could cause casualties on the water.

"I should've gone out with you," he said. "I wasn't thinking."

"I don't think Ryan would've let you," she said. "Paying customers only."

"You've got to get a different instructor."

Ash glanced at him, trying to decide if he was jealous or not. He wasn't disgruntled anymore, and it was impossible to tell why he wanted her to get someone else to teach her how to scuba dive.

"You're cute when you're jealous." Ash gave him a tiny smile, feeling an energy buzzing inside her.

"I already told you I prefer handsome." He flashed her a smile, and a moment of silence passed before they simultaneously burst into laughter.

———

NOT MUCH CHANGED OVER THE NEXT COUPLE OF WEEKS. Ash ran with Burke in the mornings. She sewed her fingers to the bone. She helped her mother in the evenings. While Burke usually spent time with her behind a closed door, they'd been going out more often. She supposed that was a big change.

And when he walked into her sewing shop the day before the wedding she'd been working, that was also new. "Lunch," he announced. He'd stopped by a few times over the last two weeks, and she supposed that had changed too.

Her feelings for him had changed too, but she wasn't sure if it was in the right direction. Because she liked him more and more. She had a feeling she'd either end up with a shattered heart or lose her best friend if she continued down this road. She didn't like either option, but she didn't see a way out of it.

He set a bowl in front of her, and the sticky, sweet scent of teriyaki sauce met her nose. "Is this a brown rice bowl?"

"With guac." He sat in a chair across from her sewing station and sighed.

She watched him for an extra moment. He looked the same as always. Maybe a bit on the tired side. Maybe like he was carrying more weight than he normally did.

"Everything okay?" She still needed to finish the beads on the shoulders and put in the zipper in the right place after the final fitting. It was an hour's worth of work, and she could take a break for a minute.

"My dad wants to go to dinner tonight. Me, you, and my parents."

Fear hit Ash right in the gut. She'd been expecting to bring her A-game to the barbecue tomorrow. In front of a lot of people, so his parents wouldn't be able to look too closely.

"I don't know if I can," she hedged, not wanting to outright lie. "The wedding is in the morning."

Burke glanced at the sewing table where the dress lay. "I'll tell him whatever you want."

She took the plastic lid off her rice bowl and found an assortment of vegetables, grilled chicken, and all that sticky sauce. Her mouth watered and she started stirring everything together.

"What do you want to do?" she asked him.

"I think we should just go. Get it over with. Then we might be able to enjoy ourselves at the barbecue."

"You don't look happy." And she really didn't like that he wanted to get anything over with, especially something between them. She felt her heart crack a little, and she was powerless to stop it.

She put a bite of chicken, rice, and guacamole in her mouth, telling herself that she shouldn't have allowed the relationship to feel so real.

It's not real, she thought, vowing to tell herself that every day until the charade ended and she could figure out how to mend her heart and still be Burke's best friend.

"I'm okay," he said. "I'm just…worried."

"About what?" She glanced up and paused when the concern in his gaze hooked her.

"You," he said, his voice a bit rough around the edges but tender in the middle. "Us. I don't want this—whatever this is—to mess up what we have." He shook his head and looked away, leaving Ash feeling shaky and uncertain inside. "I shouldn't have asked you to do this. I just need to tell my dad the truth."

And then this would be over. Ash's heart wailed at the prospect, though it would ensure that she and Burke stayed friends.

But she wanted to be more than friends with Burke.

"Let's just see how it goes tonight," she said.

"You can get away?"

"This dress will be done in an hour, tops," she said, scooping up another bite.

"I still don't have a plan for finding a girlfriend." Burke sounded broken, and Ash set aside her food. Her heart pounded in her chest, a clear warning that she needed to let him work through this problem—*his* problem—on his own.

"Why don't you date?" she asked.

Burke looked away and folded his arms over his blue polo. "You know why."

"No, I don't. You've never really said. Not out loud." Ash got up and walked over to him. "Burke, you can tell me."

He drew in a deep breath, and Ash knelt down in front of him, glad she'd worn a loose maxi dress today.

"I fell in love with a woman named—"

"Bridgette," they said together. "Go on," Ash said.

"It was bad, Ash."

She reached out and cradled his face. "Burke, you know you're a great guy, right?" Terror bolted through her that she was about to reveal too much. But she didn't care. He was her best friend, and he was in pain.

"I guess."

"Why was this break up so painful?" she asked. "I've had guys break up with me lots of times."

"You didn't love any of them." Burke met her eyes. "I was head over heels in love with her. She was everything to me. I changed everything I did for her. And she left—" He cleared his throat, the most vulnerable Ash had ever seen him.

"She left the island for a 'great opportunity' in Cancun, like our two-year relationship was nothing. Something disposable."

Ash ducked her head, breaking the connection between them. Burke was a very loyal guy, and an act like that would wound him deeply.

"Not only that, but she went with a guy named Thom, and they got married within the first six months after she'd left. I'd asked her to marry me at least a dozen times, and she kept saying she wasn't ready, that she might never want to get married, that she wasn't sure she wanted to be tied down."

Ash jerked her head back up and met his angry eyes.

"It wasn't until I saw the pictures online that I realized she just didn't want to marry *me*." He shrugged like it was no big deal, like he'd ordered a bad cup of coffee. "So I stopped dating. I don't need that in my life, you know?"

Ash nodded. "If there's someone who knows, it's me." Ash stood and returned to her chair, putting the sewing machine between them again. After all, she'd had her wedding dress sketched out and planned for two and a half decades. At this point, she didn't think she'd ever get to piece it together and sew the stitches exactly how she wanted them.

"I'll pick you up at five?" he asked, his chair scraping as he stood.

"Yeah." She didn't look up from her rice bowl, though her appetite had fled about the time he'd confessed his love for someone else. Even though it had been years ago, he was still broken up about it. How could she compete with a ghost?

"Thanks, Ash. See you later." He left and Ash left her food on the table and opened a drawer in the built-in counter. A manila folder sat there and she ran her fingertips down the side of it.

She finally took it out and opened it, the sketches and plans for her wedding dress and the entire affair were still there. The high-waisted dress would still look good on her frame, and the second sheet showed the veil she'd thought she'd wanted.

But veils were totally out at the moment, and she'd worked on her hair besides. She didn't want to cover it up.

"Doesn't matter," she said, not bothering to look at the rest of the things she'd jotted down. The cake. The altar. None of it mattered.

Because she was never going to find someone to marry.

Chapter Seven

Burke drove away from Ash's sewing studio, the sign with *Dress of Your Dreams* fading in his rear-view mirror until he couldn't read it anymore.

He had no idea what he was doing. Before the conversation with his father a couple of weeks ago, his life was simple, made up of flowers and friends and informality.

But now, he had feelings he had to face, and new feelings for Ash he didn't know how to deal with, and frustration with his father he'd never experienced before.

"And now they want to have dinner." He flipped on his turn signal a little too roughly and it bounced back to the off position. He didn't care. He turned left and headed down the highway toward the flower farm. There was always something to do there, and maybe he could drown some of his worries and irritation in the warehouse.

No matter what, Opal would put him to work. A Hawaiian woman about a foot shorter than him, Opal came with a firm tone and a smile for everything she said. Burke had always respected her, and she'd worked for their company for twenty years.

After parking and going inside the cool warehouse, he found her standing at a counter with a delivery driver. Burke hung back, listening but not intruding. The man— Kevin Diamond—finally had Opal sign the clipboard, and he turned toward Burke.

"Hey," he said, but no grin came with it.

Burke lifted his hand in a semi-wave as Kevin passed, his eyes storming with annoyance. "What's going on with him?" he asked as Kevin continued to retreat, climb in his truck, and drive away.

"We lost a shipment of flowers at the airport this morning," Opal said as if she were discussing the weather. "Kevin's sure one of his guys didn't make the pick-up, but I was here, and it was Davy."

Burke rolled his eyes. "Davy's so unreliable. Where would he possibly have taken an entire truck of flowers?"

"I have my suspicions," she said, rounding the counter.

"You think he's selling them on his own?"

"That's right. And I told Kevin he better find those flowers—and Davy—and pay us back or get our flowers to the shop at the airport." She exhaled and looked down at the large desk calendar on the counter. "Now we're behind in packaging for the overseas shipment."

"That's why I'm here," Burke said. "Put me to work."

Opal beamed up at him, her dark eyes set against her dark skin broadcasting her affection for him. "You're such a good boy, Burke."

Burke was anything but a boy these days, but he simply smiled and followed Opal toward packaging, where flowers were being placed in plastic containers and then put in boxes with dry ice. "The truck will be here in an hour, and we have all of these to do."

The scene before Burke looked like a swimming pool filled with orchids. But he pushed up his sleeves and got to work.

Unfortunately, the work wasn't taxing. Didn't require him to think that hard, and that left his brain to wander down strange roads where he held Ash's hand, kissed her, and whispered all kinds of personal things to her. Things he hadn't told anyone else.

Like what had happened with Bridgette. He wasn't sure why Ash hadn't asked before, or why he'd shared with her today. But if there was one person he trusted explicitly, it was Ash. Plus, now that they had these roles to play, she deserved to know.

A rumbling engine sounded behind him, and he hurried to box another flower. Then another. The people he worked with didn't look up. They simply worked as a couple of men started loading the boxes that were ready. The screech of tape being stretched to secure one more box rang out over and over.

"Truck's full," he finally heard, and a collective sigh

of relief went up. No, they hadn't boxed all the flowers, but that didn't matter. They needed full shipments to go out, and they'd accomplished that.

While Opal took care of the paperwork for the shipment of flowers heading by plane to Oahu, Burke looked around at the rest of the people, who continued to box flowers. "We're doing them all?" he asked the man nearest him.

Jorge said, "Yeah, another plane tomorrow. They'll keep in the fridge." His fingers moved with quick strokes, always on target.

Burke got back to work, half-hoping that this job would make it impossible for him to eat with his parents.

You really need to figure out what to do about Ash.

Because he could tell his dad the truth—that he'd thrown out Ash's name on a whim, when they weren't dating. But the last two weeks with her had been...different. And a good kind of different.

The kind of different Burke wanted. He just hadn't known it. He liked going out with Ash instead of just hiding inside her house. Liked holding her hand as they walked down the beach as the sun set into the water. Liked it when other men looked at them like he'd gotten a prize they wanted.

He liked listening to her talk about her scuba diving lessons, and ask him questions about his flower farm, and detail how her mother was doing.

I like Ash, he thought, and while he'd admitted it out loud to her only a few hours ago, he now knew that it was a romantic kind of like and not just a best friend like.

Could she ever think of him as her real boyfriend?

He thought about the question as he finished boxing the last of the orchids. As he showered and drove to her cottage. When she answered the door wearing the same flowing, flowery dress she'd had on while she sewed, Burke's heart did a little breakdance inside his chest.

"Hey," he breathed, maybe a little too much emotion in his voice. He wanted to sweep into her personal space, wrap his arms around her, and press a kiss to her temple.

He reminded himself that she was his *best* friend, not his *girl*friend, and that he'd fallen way too fast in the past.

He wasn't going to do that again. Even if he found the courage to tell Ash about his new feelings for her, he wasn't going to give her his whole heart at once. He'd done that before, and Bridgette had given it back to him in pieces. In fact, he suspected some shards of it were strewn from here to Cancun and he'd never get them all back.

"Why are you staring at me like that?" Ash ran her hand over her hair self-consciously. "Too much makeup?"

Burke blinked and drank in the beauty of her face. Those wide, dark eyes, the curls that fell just below her shoulders, the bronze skin that said she spent a lot of time in the sun when really she didn't. Her father had simply been Hawaiian and given her his coloring.

"You look great," he managed to say.

"I didn't have time to change. Your Tidal Forever called me over for a consultation this afternoon, and I ended up signing another bride."

"That's good, though, right?" He offered her his arm, which felt like a simple step down the boyfriend lane.

She stared at it for a moment and then lifted her eyes to his before slipping her hand along his forearm. "It's good, yes. It's a January wedding too, which is pretty rare around here."

"True. People tend to book for Christmas, right?"

"Burke, I had no idea you listened to me when I babble on about my work."

Burke laughed and tightened his arm against his body. "Of course I do."

"Well, I can barely tell you what you grow up on that farm of yours."

"Oh, I barely know that."

She laughed with him, and Burke felt like they could definitely take their relationship out of the friend zone. Easily.

His throat went dry when he thought about kissing Ash. Sure, he'd entertained the idea years ago—many, many years ago, when they were both still teenagers.

But her brother Leo had squashed that idea right out of his head. Burke wondered what Leo would say now, and his gut twisted when he remembered that Leo and his whole family would be coming to the barbecue tomorrow, because his wife worked in the Petals and Leis human resources department.

"I think you should get a dating app," Ash said as he started his car and eased onto the road.

"A dating app?"

"To meet someone," she said. "It's low-key, and you can do as much or as little as you want." She shrugged. "You know, like send messages, or ignore them. Whatever you want. Sometimes it's freeing to be able to just talk without the pressure of being together."

He cut her a glance out of the corner of his eye. "Have you used an app before?"

"Yes," she said. "I just changed my status back to available on Get Together." She drew in a deep breath. "I need to move on from Milo too. I figured maybe you and I could figure out how to move on together."

Burke frowned, quite sure he didn't want her dating anyone new. "Why did you like that guy anyway?"

"He was…."

"An idiot," Burke said.

"I know you didn't like him. But he was different in private."

"And that's a problem, don't you think?"

"Is it?" She turned toward him fully. "*You're* different in private, Burke. You realize that, right? Who you are while lying on my couch is the complete opposite of what everyone else on this island thinks about you."

Burke opened his mouth to argue, defend himself, but found he had nothing to say. "Point taken." He pulled into the restaurant parking lot where they'd be meeting his parents and took the car out of gear. "Are you ready for this?"

"I guess so." Their eyes met for a brief moment, but Burke didn't let himself gaze at her for too long. Number one, he didn't trust himself not to reveal too much, and number two, they were already a few minutes late. His father did not like to be kept waiting.

He took Ash's hand in his as she joined him at the front of the car, and they walked into the open-air restaurant together. Misters hung high in the trees to keep people cool, and the scent of fruit filled the air.

"They're over there." He nodded toward the corner of the restaurant and led Ash toward his mom and dad. Every cell in his body quaked, but he gathered up all the wit and bravery he had.

He could do this. After all, he liked Ash and wished he was brave enough to tell her about his recent revelations about her.

"Hey, Dad. Mom."

They both stood and Burke gave his mom a quick kiss on the cheek. "You both know Ash, I think. Ash, my mom, Heather and my dad, George."

"Of course," Ash said in the tone she used on new clients. "We've met before."

"You look lovely," his mom said while his dad simply shook Ash's hand and sat back down.

After a few seconds where everyone got settled at the table, his dad asked, "So you two are serious, huh?"

"Dad, I never said we were serious." Burke wanted to reach under the table and squeeze Ash's hand. "I said—"

"We're not serious?" Ash asked, interrupting him.

His eyes flew to hers, searching. Needing to find an answer without having to ask a question verbally. "Well…." He had no idea what to say.

"He practically proposed the other night." Ash grinned like they were sharing secrets at this table and picked up her water glass. "Or maybe I misread him."

With both of his parent's eyes on him, Burke felt like a rubber band had been wound around his neck. "No," he said. "I was serious."

The conversation in question had never happened, but his parents didn't know that.

"So you're engaged?" his mother asked.

A long beat of silence descended on the table, the tropical music the only sound between the four of them.

"No," he heard Ash say at the same time he said, "Yeah, we're engaged."

Chapter Eight

Ash stared at Burke, not caring that his parents sat a few feet away on the other side of the table. His mom had gasped and she might have said something, but Ash couldn't process it.

Burke blinked back at her, his expression as charged as her whole body. She really wished they could escape for a minute and talk.

This is your fault, a voice whispered. She'd brought up how they were serious, when Burke was trying to downplay the relationship. Maybe she'd lost her mind. Or maybe she was tired of pretending to be his girlfriend, all while pretending not to like him.

Both charades were exhausting.

She knew she didn't like that he'd been about to say they weren't that serious, and she'd blurted out some ridiculous thing about a phantom engagement conversation.

"I just need to get her a ring," Burke said, his voice barely loud enough to reach Ash's ears. He tore his gaze from hers and focused on his parents. "She's been really busy with a dress for a wedding tomorrow. I think after that, we'll have time to go over to the jeweler."

Ash put a smile on her face. Burke sounded flawless, like everything that had happened in the last five minutes was true.

Five minutes.

How had so much changed in such a small amount of time?

Thankfully, the waiter arrived and took drink orders. The conversation moved to the barbecue and business, and Ash did her best to stay engaged, look interested, and participate. George kept looking at her with a sharpness in his eyes she didn't like, but he never said anything. Didn't question why they'd started dating when they'd been friends for so long.

Once, he said, "So, Ash," and Heather had put her hand over his.

"How's your mom?" she'd asked, clearly not the question George was going to use.

The meal went quickly, and before she knew it, George put down enough money for everyone's dinner and said, "Sorry to cut things short. I have to be in the fields early." He looked at Burke. "You too, right?"

"Right," Burke said, but he stayed in his seat while his father and mother rose.

Ash stood and gave Heather a tiny hug and George a

great big smile. Burke finally got up and said goodbye to his parents, and then he sank back into his seat as they walked away.

Ash sipped her soda, the carbonation sliding down her throat causing zings and pins to race over her skin. She waited until his parents left the restaurant completely, and then she hissed, "Engaged?"

Burke leaned closer to her, his eyes blazing. "You're the one who said we were serious. I was going to tell them the truth!"

Ash couldn't decide if he was upset or not. Okay, he was definitely upset, but she wasn't sure if it was because the situation had worsened or because of what she'd said. It didn't matter. What she'd said had made the situation worse.

"What were you thinking?" he asked next, some of the fight leaving his posture.

"I don't know," she said.

"We don't lie to each other." His bright blue eyes flashed with fire and he picked up his cola.

I like you sounded inside her head. Could she just say it?

She'd already said it.

Desperation made her voice tight when she said, "Okay, so, maybe I just didn't want…."

This to end.

"…You to have to deal with him alone." That sounded like a bestie thing to say.

"I can deal with him."

"You don't want to lose Petals and Leis, do you?"

"Of course not."

"Then we're serious and you better find me a ring to wear in the next week or so." She drained the last of her soda and started to stand.

Burke put his hand on her arm, making her pause and sit down again. "Ash." He said her name with so much emotion in his voice she couldn't identify all the pieces of it.

She looked at him and he looked at her, and he finally said, "Thank you." He tipped forward like he might kiss her, and Ash's hopes went wild. Her eyes drifted partway closed, and everything went silent.

His breath wafted across her cheek, her chin, and just when she thought she should check and make sure he wasn't teasing her, his lips touched hers.

Ash expected all the fantasies she'd been having the past few months to suddenly pale in comparison to what actually kissing Burke was like.

But it was just a touch. His lips felt hot against hers and while her heart was thrumming like hummingbird wings, and she wanted to kiss him, he ended up pulling away without really *kissing* her.

It had just been a touching of lips. Not a kiss.

Embarrassment raced through her, especially when Burke stood up and said, "We should go." Since the bill had already been paid, he simply stood, tossed his napkin on the table, and turned toward the exit.

Ash sat at the table for a minute, dumbfounded.

Never in her wildest dreams had she thought kissing Burke would be bad.

But that definitely hadn't been good.

She launched to her feet, determined to try again before he drove away from her cottage. Maybe he was just out of practice. After all, he hadn't dated anyone in six years. She caught up to him, and the drive back to her cottage happened with the low strains of the radio filling the silence between them.

When he didn't get out of the car to walk her to the door, panic wedged itself in between Ash's heartbeats.

"Are you okay?" she asked.

"Tonight was a disaster," he said, staring straight ahead.

A squeak came out of Ash's mouth, and she felt like he'd just punched the air from her lungs. She couldn't imagine walking inside and letting him drive away with things as they were between them. She'd never be able to fall asleep, and everything would be ten shades of awkward at the barbecue tomorrow.

Maybe they wouldn't go to the barbecue tomorrow.

Sitting in Burke's car, Ash felt more defeated than she ever had. Yes, she'd known she'd never leave the island from a very young age. She'd known she'd design and sew wedding dresses for a living.

She'd always enjoyed dating and having a boyfriend, but nothing had ever stuck.

The real question is, are you willing to sacrifice your friendship with Burke for a chance at something more? she thought.

Immediately, her voice of reason countered with, *What if it doesn't work out? Do you think you can just go back to being friends?*

Ash honestly didn't know the answer to either question, but she'd been trying to change how she did things. Try new opportunities. Get outside her circle of comfort.

She turned toward Burke and drew in a deep breath. "Burke, I want to try that kiss again."

He swung his attention toward her, a storm making his handsome features dark and dangerous. Confusion swept through his eyes, and Ash reached over, completely unsure of what she was doing, but doing it anyway.

She cradled his face and said, "I like you, Burke. Like, I have this strange little crush on you, and I don't know… maybe if you could see me as your girlfriend at all…." She trailed off, wishing he'd jump in and say something.

Anything.

"I mean, I know we've been friends for a long time and all that." She cleared her throat and dropped her hand. The car was suddenly ten times too small. "But I'm tired of pretending." She reached for the door handle. "I like you, and maybe sometime in the future, we can try that kiss again."

She got out of the car as quickly as she could, slammed the door behind her, and almost ran to her front door. She half-expected Burke to call after her or come after her, but he did neither. She went inside the house and locked the door before pressing her back into the wood.

She breathed in. She breathed out.

"Nothing more to do now," she muttered, refusing to peek out the window to see if Burke still sat in his car or not.

————

"WHAT ARE YOU DOING HERE?" CHARLOTTE DANE POKED her head out of her office as Ash started to pass it. "I heard the door open, and I didn't think anyone was coming in today."

Ash wanted to rush right into Charlotte's office and tell her everything. Instead she stood in the hall, anxiety attacking her on several levels. She liked Charlotte. She was one of the best new additions to Your Tidal Forever, and she'd brought Ash eleven new clients in the eighteen months she'd been on the island.

The scent of peaches and flowers filled the air here, one of the owner's favorite scents. Hope had candles burning in every room when she was in the office, but today, it was just Charlotte.

Who was still watching her.

Ash sighed. "I was just going to go over the master calendar." She did like looking at the huge wall that detailed everything going on at Your Tidal Forever. Hope was nothing if not detailed, and she had someone who managed the calendar full-time.

She stepped that way, unsurprised when Charlotte

followed her. Today, Charlotte wore a simple pair of cutoffs and a purple tank top. "When's the barbecue?"

"I don't know. Noon, probably."

"You don't know?"

Ash turned a corner and the calendar came into view. "Burke hasn't texted me yet."

"There's something wrong," Charlotte said, and Ash turned toward her.

"The calendar looks right to me."

"With you," Charlotte said, a gentle smile easing onto her face. "I've known you for a while, Ash. You're always polished and put together. You know the calendar forward and backward, and you know exactly what time the barbecue starts."

Ash felt shaky from head to toe, and she really wished her bottom lip would stop quaking. "How good are you at keeping secrets?"

"Oh, I'm the best," she said, making an X over her heart. "In fact, I have something I've been keeping to myself for a few weeks now."

Ash peered at her with interest. "What is it?"

"You first." Charlotte settled her weight on her back foot and folded her arms. "You look…distressed."

"It's a very long story."

"I came in to get a little peace and quiet," she said. "I've got nothing but time."

"Well, then let's not stand in the hall. Is there any coffee here?"

"No, but I have chocolate in my office."

Ash followed Charlotte back down the halls and into one of the larger offices at Your Tidal Forever. She pushed a bag of chocolate covered sea salt caramels toward Ash. "Take your time. Dawson's flying today, and we have roofers at our place, so it's noisy. I'm not really working. More like pushing paper around."

Ash took a handful of the perfectly round caramels and put one in her mouth. Sweet and salty and chocolatly, she definitely needed to get some of these for herself.

"They make guava ones too," Charlotte said. "The fruity caramel is divine with the chocolate."

"These are fantastic." Ash checked the bag and found the trademark Alvey's A on it, which had an extra-long slash through the middle of the letter, with tropical flowers on the left end. Belinda Alvey was a couple of years older than Ash, and another Getaway Bay native.

"I love their mint sandwich crèmes," she said. "But I haven't had these."

"They have a new shop over on Market Street," Charlotte said as if Ash had dropped by to chat about candy. "Belinda said these are new within the last month."

Ash popped another one in her mouth, relishing the melty way every flavor played together. "Well, they're great."

Charlotte smiled and went back to a particularly large blueprint she was working on.

Ash finished her handful of chocolate and let out another sigh. "Have I told you about Burke?"

"Sure, Burke Lawson. Running partner. Best friend. Couch crasher."

"I like him," Ash blurted. "Like I want to be his girlfriend, and he told his dad I was his girlfriend, and we've been pretending, but I haven't been pretending, but then he kissed me and it was awful."

She sucked at the air, misery rushing in where her nerves had been previously.

Charlotte stared at her. "What?"

Ash pushed her hair off her face and told the whole story, slower and in more complete sentences. "And I told him last night that I liked him, like for real, and wanted to kiss him again," she finished. "And he hasn't called or texted in almost fourteen hours."

Her eyes grew hot, but she would not cry. Not over a bad kiss. Not over Burke ignoring her. She mentally went through her stock of buttons and notions until her emotions calmed and she could look at Charlotte.

"He'll call," she said.

"We're supposed to go to the barbecue and pretend," she said. "I don't know how long he'll want to keep it up. I know he doesn't want to lose his farm."

"Do you think his father would really do that?"

Ash thought of George's stern expression from last night, the question he'd been about to ask. "You know what? I do. And Burke would be devastated."

She couldn't believe she'd told him to join an online

dating site. She didn't want him to do that. Didn't want to sprint down the beach with him while he talked about how wonderful his real girlfriend was.

She also couldn't see Kayla or Krista running Petals and Leis. His younger sisters were her age, and she knew they worked at the family flower farm. But running it? That had always been Burke. He'd gotten two degrees to do it. Worked from before dawn to dusk.

And Ash would do whatever he needed her to do to make sure he got his farm. The thought of him rejecting her and keeping up the ruse until he found someone else made her stomach twist. But she'd do it.

Her phone made a strange notification sound she didn't recognize, and she looked at the screen. *You have a new message from—*

The message from Get Together, the dating app she'd used in the past cut off the name of the person. She cursed herself for activating her account again and setting herself as single and ready to mingle.

She didn't want to get together with anyone except Burke. She wasn't interested in a long-distance relationship, as the Pacific Ocean was bigger than most men bargained for. Ash swiped open the message anyway to find someone who hadn't even put a picture in their profile circle yet. So a green, empty head stared back at her while she studied the screen name.

Petals4Burke

"Oh my heck," she said, her words made mostly of

air. "Burke just sent me a message through my dating app." She glanced up at Charlotte, who grinned at her.

"Well, read it out loud," she said.

Ash tapped on the message and read it quickly before giving it voice. "Hey, Ash. Thought we could connect on here, seeing as how you're single and I'm single."

She looked up and met Charlotte's eye. "I don't get it."

"Message him back," Charlotte said. "He obviously has something to say."

"What do I even say?" Ash had never been more grateful to run into someone when she'd been hoping to be alone.

"Start with…."

Chapter Nine

*A*re you sure you're single? Your status says undetermined.

Burke stared at Ash's message, his chest loosening now that she'd responded. He had her phone number, and he could go to her house. But he'd tossed and turned last night, her words reverberating around inside his head and keeping him awake.

I'm tired of pretending.

Maybe we can try that kiss again.

Embarrassment and humiliation had been constant companions since that terrible kiss in the restaurant. It was like Burke had forgotten how to kiss a woman he liked.

He'd tried making excuses for himself until about midnight. Everything from *It's been a long time since I kissed someone* to *It was unexpected. I was nervous.*

He tapped around on the app, finally finding the place that he could choose his relationship status. He chose single and navigated back to the messages. Ash had been very easy to find on Get Together, mostly because he'd searched by location.

AshyGirl was typing, and a message popped up that said *I heard a rumor that you're actually engaged.*

His parents weren't going to ever check this app, and Burke wanted things to be real with Ash. She'd been real with him last night, and while it left him discombobulated and a bit uncomfortable, he wanted to do the same for her.

The barbecue is at three, he typed out and sent. *I was hoping you might want to get together for lunch before we go.*

Won't we be eating at the barbecue?

Burke sighed as frustration built inside him. *I'll buy you as much coffee as you want.* Did he sound desperate to see her? Probably. But he'd been thinking about that failed kiss and what a second one might be like. He wanted to see her, find out if the attraction between them was that electric pulsing that had been firing in his pulse for a couple of weeks now.

He wasn't sure what he'd do if it wasn't, or if their second kiss was as bad as the first. He just knew he wanted to find out—and that was something he hadn't wanted to do since Bridgette.

He closed the app before Ash could respond, and he called her. She answered with, "I'll meet you at Sea Party in twenty minutes. I want to start with the vanilla mocha Frappuccino."

"Twenty minutes," Burke said, and if they were still

in best friend status, they'd both hang up and see each other in twenty minutes. But neither of them ended the call this time.

"I'm sorry," Burke blurted.

"About what?"

"The only thing that was a disaster last night was that kiss, which I'd totally like a do-over on."

Silence poured through the line, and Burke checked to make sure the call was still connected. It was, and Ash came on, along with some background noise, which meant she'd covered the mouthpiece of her phone for a moment.

"All right," Ash said. "Apology accepted. See you in twenty minutes." She hung up, but not before Burke heard at least two women giggling, and an added measure of embarrassment pulled through him.

"Doesn't matter," he told himself. "You're going to go meet her and find a way to tell her that you have a little crush on her too, and maybe you'll have to keep pretending but that maybe the engagement could be real too."

He shook his head. He was deluding himself if he thought he was ready to be engaged, even to Ash. Heck, two weeks ago, he hadn't even been ready to start dating.

His phone bleeped out a weird little chime, and he checked it. Someone else had friended him on Get Together, a woman named Darcy Hinkle. A groan started in the back of his throat and ground out across his vocal cords.

No, he was definitely not interested in Darcy, or being on this app, and he uninstalled it before leaving to go meet Ash at Sea Party.

———

THIRTY MINUTES LATER, HER VANILLA MOCHA Frappuccino was cold and his coffee was gone. As were an order of lobster fritters.

"Ginger spiced sea scallops," the waitress said as she set another plate in front of him. "Do you want another long macchiato?"

"Yes, please." He handed over his cup, and the brunette disappeared. His leg tapped, and he wondered if he'd have to sit through another cup of coffee before Ash showed up.

He'd just sliced a scallop in half when the chair across from his scraped against the concrete. "Sorry I'm late."

Burke stared at Ash. Her curls fell over her shoulders in easy waves, and she pushed them back in that self-conscious way she had. Their eyes met, and that electricity leapt from her to him, jumpstarting his heart and making the way he pushed her coffee toward her clumsy.

"It's cold," he said instead of hello. He pulled in a breath through his nose and said, "It's good to see you. I thought for a minute you wouldn't show up." He added a nervous chuckle, and Ash smiled as she lifted her cup to her lips.

A tiny sip, and she grimaced, put the cup down, and crossed her arms over her chest. The waitress returned with his macchiato, and he said, "She needs a new vanilla mocha."

"No problem." She collected the offending drink and walked away.

Burke figured he had a few minutes before the Frappuccino returned, and he didn't want to beat around the bush. "So you have a little crush on me?"

He regretted the words as soon as they left his mouth. Arrogant much?

"At least I don't totally want a do-over of that kiss. If you can even call it that." She glared at him, adding a smile the longer they watched one another.

Burke started laughing, her remark deserved. When she joined in, all the tension between them broke. "So are we really going to give things a try?" he asked.

The waitress put Ash's new coffee on the table and made herself scarce. Ash picked up her cup and took a sip, a smile warming her whole face. "We're already pretending. If it doesn't work out, we'll just break up like we've always planned." She sounded nonchalant about the whole thing, but Burke didn't buy it for a second.

Ash was the type of woman who planned and prepared. She probably knew what she'd be doing a month from now. But he said, "All right," and reached across the table to gently take her hand in his, his head ducked and his eyes focused on the table.

"I started feeling things for you when I held your hand a few weeks ago," he said really quietly.

"You've never felt anything for me before?" she asked.

He lifted his gaze to hers. "Well, when I was younger. In high school. Leo made it quite clear you were off-limits." And Burke was fairly certain her older brother's opinions hadn't changed.

A sourness filled Ash's expression. "Leo? He said something to you?"

"Yes," Burke said. "And he probably still would."

"Why? I'm thirty-five-years-old." She cocked her head. "And you were his best friend. Why would he think we shouldn't be together?"

Burke shrugged. "I don't know."

"We don't lie to each other," she said.

Burke sighed, half amused she'd used his words against him and half annoyed. "Fine. He didn't think we'd last, and he didn't want you to get hurt."

Ash's eyes blazed, and she reached for her phone. "Oh, I'm going to talk to him about this."

Burke covered her hand with his. "It's not worth it, Ash."

Their eyes met again, and Burke wondered if now would be a good time for that kiss do-over.

Nope, he thought. *Not in another restaurant.* He wanted to kiss her when he was all alone with her, so he could take as much time as he needed to truly experience her and let her know how he felt.

He looked away, and said, "So we're pretending, but not pretending."

"Well, the engagement is still fake," she said.

That was for dang sure, but Burke kept the thought to himself. He'd proposed so many times to Bridgette, he'd actually vowed never to do it again. If the relationship with Ash progressed that much, would he even be able to get the words out?

If things get that serious with Ash, he thought. You'll be over Bridgette and ready to move on.

Burke seized onto that thought, because he really wanted to move on. Had for a while. Hadn't known how. But with Ash by his side, he thought it might actually be possible.

————

Burke held Ash's hand as they walked into the gardens at Aloha Hideaway. It was cool in the shade, and there were misters like at the restaurant the other night. Long tables had been set up, and they held huge, stainless steel buffet servers. The scent of pineapple and roasted meat hung in the air, almost distracting Burke from the sight of his father speaking to a red-headed woman.

He led Ashley in that direction in time to catch the end of the conversation and to say hello to Stacey DuPont, the owner of Aloha Hideaway. She'd grown up on the island too, and while she was a few years older than Burke, it seemed like all the island natives knew each other.

She'd inherited this building and land from her grandfather, and Burke felt a kinship with her for that reason.

"She's bringing out the rolls, and then we'll start," his dad said.

Everyone knew Burke's mother planned these barbecues, but his dad would be the one to say a few words of acknowledgement and gratitude for their company and employees. Then they'd eat, and play games, and enjoy the beach. Later that night, there'd be fireworks and brownies, and his father would have a bonus check for everyone who worked for the company.

"Great," Burke said. "I'm starving." Three cups of coffee was not food, and even the fritters and scallops were hours ago.

"Have you two gotten a ring yet?"

"Dad, I said it would be a few days." Burke tightened his hand in Ash's. "Dinner was just last night." It seemed impossible that less than twenty-four hours had passed since then. A lifetime of things had happened with Ash, and she squeezed his hand back, grounding him.

He moved away from his dad, but he didn't go far. If he was going to take over the farm—and thus the barbecues—in the future, he'd need to be seen by the employees. Earn their respect.

But you do that at work, he told himself. *Not a barbecue.*

So he migrated further over to the cooler with the

strawberry orange punch and got some for himself and Ash. He turned back to the crowd and did a sweeping glance of everyone there. A few more people came into the gardens, and then Stacey returned with two other people and set the rolls on the end of one of the tables.

She nodded to Burke's father, and he said, "Welcome," in his great booming voice. "Heather and I are so glad you could all make it to our annual barbecue this summer." He beamed around at everyone, even the people behind him. If there was one thing about his dad, he was charismatic and commanding. Burke would give him that.

"This is our second year at Aloha Hideaway, but in case any of you don't remember, Stacey makes the best Kalua pork on the island." He flashed her a smile. "And today, we have homemade sweet buns from down the beach at Sweet Breeze Resort and Spa, which she also owns."

Burke wasn't sure why he was mentioning Sweet Breeze, but he really wanted one of those homemade buns. He'd read an Internet article about them, and the Hawaiian woman who'd been hired at the resort and then introduced them to the menu. Apparently, tourists and locals alike went to the hotel to eat just because of the buns.

"Today, I'd like to thank each and every one of you for the dedication and hours you put in at Petals and Leis. We're up twelve percent in revenue this year, our highest gain in a decade."

Applause broke out, and Burke released Ash's hand in order to clap. He spotted Leo and his wife coming down the path and further into the gardens, and he tensed. But Leo didn't scan the crowd for him, and why should he?

"And I'd like to make one announcement before we eat. Petals and Leis has just inked a new agreement with both Sweet Breeze Resort and Spa in Getaway Bay and the Ohana Resort in the East Bay. We'll be their sole flower supplier and have kiosks in their lobbies for lei and flower sales." His smile reached the very edges of the party, and probably beyond.

A cheer went up, and Burke couldn't help the pride swelling in his chest. He'd suggested kiosks in Getaway Bay and other big tourist places, and his father had started with the two biggest resorts on the island.

But still. It felt good that one of his ideas had some merit in his father's eyes—*and* it would help their company grow.

"All right." His father held up both hands, laughter in his words and on his face. "We've got food now. Festivities will begin shortly, and we've got access to Aloha Hideaway's private beach until midnight. Fireworks and bonuses will be around nine-thirty, and Stacey's provided us with a popcorn bar this year too. That'll be set up at seven." He met her eyes, and she nodded.

"So let's eat!"

People immediately moved toward the buffet set up on the tables, but Burke hung back. Ash stayed right at his side, her slender fingers slipping right back between his. A thrill ran down his back, and he glanced at her.

"Thanks for doing this," he said.

"Don't thank me yet," she said, nodding toward something. "Here comes Leo, and I'm going to give him a piece of my mind."

Chapter Ten

Ash watched as Leo took in her and Burke standing together—not uncommon. Maybe she'd never come to his company barbecue before, but this year things were different.

He realized she was holding hands when he was about ten paces away, and all of his features darkened. She felt something inside her boiling too, and she narrowed her eyes at him.

"Hey," he said as he approached and then stopped. "What's going on here?" At least he wasn't interested in beating around the bush.

"Nothing," Ash said. "Where'd Genevieve go with the kids?" Ash loved her nephew and her niece, and they loved her too.

"Brooklyn had to go to the bathroom, so Gen took them both in so we could eat afterward."

"Yeah, we're just waiting too," Burke said. "The line'll die down soon enough."

"You're holding her hand."

"She is standing right here," Ash said, stepping forward. "And it's none of your business who I date, Leo."

His eyebrows stretched toward the sky. "Date?"

"I can't *believe* you told him to stay away from me."

"You were sixteen. He was too old for you." Leo didn't apologize for much, and Ash honestly wasn't expecting him to do so now.

"I'm definitely old enough to make my own decisions now," she said. "So you don't get to say anything."

Leo looked like he might argue, but Theo called, "Daddy, come eat!" and he turned in the direction of his five-year-old son.

He turned back to Ash, his dark eyes softening. He looked so much like their father that Ash felt like she could have him back sometimes. "I'll check on Mom tonight," he said. "We won't be able to stay all night with the kids anyway." He glanced at Burke and back at Ash. "Then you two can stay here. We'll come back for the fireworks."

"Thank you, Leo," Ash said, her anger and frustration with her brother draining away.

Burke relaxed with every step Leo took away from them, and Ash did too. But when he leaned down, his lips practically touching her ear, she tensed again. "You didn't say we were engaged?"

The question in his tone made her turn toward him, and their faces were now only inches apart. She gazed into those oceanic eyes, and let herself dive into them. "Shoot. I forgot about the engagement."

"He probably won't say anything to my dad," Burke said. "It's Genevieve who works for us."

Ash nodded, her eyes falling to Burke's mouth. She wondered what it would be like to truly be kissed by him. Have him actually *kiss* her instead of just holding his lips against hers. The temperature in the garden rose by a dozen degrees, and he leaned a bit closer to her.

She cleared her throat. "Not happening in front of all your employees," she murmured, and the man backed up.

"Right." He gave himself a little shake and tugged on her hand as he started walking toward the buffet line. "Well, if I can't kiss you, the second best thing would be to eat. I'm starving."

Ash laughed, because surely he couldn't be that hungry. He'd eaten a whole order of lobster fritters by himself only a few hours ago. But he loaded his plate with three Hawaiian sweet buns, two scoops of Kalua pork, and more baked beans than he could possibly eat.

Ash basked in the sound of people laughing and talking, the scent of delicious meat and bread and tropical fruits, and the feel of the man beside her. This was definitely the best Fourth of July she'd had in her whole life, and as the games started, she found a chair near a tree to just watch, Burke's hand in hers.

AN HOUR LATER, ASH SAT ONLY A FEW INCHES OFF THE sand. She'd come out to the beach with Theo and Brooklyn and helped them build a sandcastle while their parents got a few minutes of relaxation time.

Burke said, "If you do that, it'll get too wet and collapse."

Theo looked at him, said nothing, and dug the moat the way he wanted. He ran down to the shore and filled the bucket with water while Ash braided Brooklyn's hair. "It's going to fall," she whispered to the little girl.

Theirs wasn't the only sand castle on the private beach, but it was definitely the best. Burke had clearly spent a lot of time constructing castles, and Theo had been enamored with him from the very first bucketful of sand.

Theo came back up the beach slower than he'd gone down it, the weight of the water in the bucket obvious. He tipped it into the moat and everything seemed like it was going to be okay.

He grinned at Burke, who laughed from where he lay on his side. "Good job, buddy."

"Brooklyn, Theo, it's time to go." Gen came through the gate that led into the Hideaway gardens, but neither of her children went over to her.

"Mom, I'm not done with the castle." Theo poured some more water into the moat he'd dug, and sand started caving away on the side.

"Watch out," Burke said, and Theo started packing more sand onto the weakened part.

"Now," Gen said. "We have to go visit Grandma, and then we'll come back for the fireworks."

At that moment, the scent of popcorn met Ash's nose, and she turned to see Stacey and Fisher bringing out huge bowls of the stuff. Her stomach growled though she'd eaten plenty for dinner.

Still, that had been a few hours ago, and there wouldn't be dinner tonight—unless she could get Burke to go around the curve in the bay to the taco stand that had sprung up next to the shaved ice place.

"I want popcorn," Brooklyn said in quite the whiny voice.

"We'll take some on the way out." Gen lifted Brooklyn off Ash's lap. "Thanks, Ash. Will you save us a spot for the fireworks?"

"Of course."

"See, Aunty Ashy is going to save us a spot. We'll just be gone for a couple of hours." Gen flashed a smile at Brooklyn and then Ash. "Go see if Daddy will get you some popcorn." She turned to Theo. "Come on, bud."

He furiously put more sand on the side of the castle, but the water had done its damage, as Burke had said it would.

"Theo," Gen warned, and he finally stood, his hands coated in wet sand.

"Fine," he said. "It's going to fall anyway."

"I'll fix it up for us," Burke said. "Okay?"

"Okay," Theo said, and he ran over to Leo too. Gen looked back and forth between Ash and Burke, her mind clearly spinning.

"You two are cute together. I'm not sure what Leo's problem is."

"He prefers handsome," Ash said, throwing a smile in Burke's direction. "But thanks. I kinda like him."

Burke just gazed at her with this look of wonder on his face that she couldn't quite decipher. Gen turned to go, adding, "I'll keep the engagement on the down-low."

Before Ash could respond, her sister-in-law left. Burke looked at her and they started laughing together. He came over and positioned a beach chair beside her.

"Before you sit down, could you get me some popcorn?" She looked up at him, and though she wore sunglasses, she felt sure he could see her puppy dog eyes. "Please? I love popcorn. Cheese and caramel and plain. With extra salt if they have it on the table."

Burke blinked at her. "Popcorn. Cheese and caramel and plain. With extra salt." He saluted and walked away, leaving Ash to wonder if she should tell him that popcorn was her love language.

Bring her some of that, and he might as well take her heart too.

In the end, she accepted her very favorite snack and kept her mouth shut as the sun sank lower and lower in the sky.

When dusk settled, they folded up their chairs and stacked them against the low wall separating the garden from the beach. Burke got two blankets from the stack and spread them out side-by-side before lying back on one.

He rested his weight on his elbows and forearms and gazed up at the sky. Ash perched on the blanket beside him, her legs criss-crossed in front of her. She wanted to cuddle into him, but it wasn't quite dark enough yet and she didn't want to put on a show for anyone.

"My dad loved the stars," she said, training her gaze into the heavens too.

"I can see why," he said. "The moon is beautiful tonight."

She glanced at him, finding him beautiful tonight. She couldn't believe she was there with him and that this was real.

Not all of it. Of course, the rational side of her was ever-present, correcting her whenever she allowed herself to get a little too wrapped up in her fantasies.

The engagement wasn't real, and she had no guarantees the relationship would even last.

Then what?

It doesn't matter, she told herself. She wanted to enjoy her time with Burke, not second-guess everything he did. He'd said he had feelings for her. Sure, they might be new, but they were there. She could see them in his eyes, feel it in his touch as his fingers drifted across hers and then held on.

"Come lay by me," he said, his voice on the outer edge of a whisper.

She did, glad for the cover of darkness on this hot July night. She felt like she fit right against Burke's chest, and she inhaled the scent of sunscreen and sweat from his skin, finding him sexy and safe.

She didn't want to lose herself to too many moments, though. She'd felt this way inside the circle of Milo's arms too, and he'd turned out to be one of her biggest mistakes. He had been different in private, but she should've known something was off about him when literally every single friend of hers didn't like him.

But people liked Burke just fine, and Ash felt herself slipping a little bit more as someone set up a speaker system and started broadcasting in the Getaway Bay feed for the patriotic songs.

Burke traced an unknown pattern on her bare arm, making her shiver. "You cold?" he asked, his voice husky and making her feel melty inside.

"No," she said, not wanting him to know the full effect he had on her. "Just thinking about more popcorn."

He chuckled, his chest vibrating against her back. "You ate like a gallon of that stuff."

"Probably two." She laughed with him, seriously considering kissing him right here on this blanket, at his company party.

Then she heard, "Aunt Ash? Where are you?" in the cutest little girl voice possible.

She retreated from Burke, sat up, and said, "Over here, guys."

There was still enough light for her brother and his family to pick their way through the blankets to the one she and Burke had saved for them.

Leo stopped on the edge of her blanket and extended something toward her. "Ice cream," he said. "From Mom's. She's doing pretty good tonight. She said she'd sit on her back porch and watch the fireworks."

A pang of guilt hit Ash. She should've gone up into the hills to her childhood home and sat on the back porch with her mother as the bright lights exploded in the sky. "Yeah? She looked like she'd eaten enough? I just put a lot of leftovers in the fridge from a couple of days ago."

She hadn't gone to see her mom last night, because of the dinner with Burke and his parents. She made a mental vow to go first thing in the morning and make sure her mom was okay.

"Yeah, she said she'd had plenty." Leo stepped past her and Burke to the blanket where his family had settled.

Ash unwrapped her ice cream bar, the sweet chill of chocolate on her tongue welcome in this muggy night. "Want some?" she asked, holding it out to Burke, who'd also sat up.

"I'm okay." He watched her eat it though; she could feel his eyes even through the thickening darkness.

She finished her treat and said, "I'm ready for this to start."

His phone brightened for a moment, illuminating that handsome face, and he said, "It's almost ten."

Feeling brave and completely out of her element with her best friend, Ash inched closer to Burke until he put his arm around her. She leaned further into his body, wanting to hold onto this moment for a long, long time.

The song on the radio ended, and the broadcaster said, "It's time to light up the Hawaiian sky," and a new tune began to play.

Within seconds, red, white, and blue sparks exploded in the sky, causing a chorus of oohs and ahhs among the people on the beach.

Burke lay back down, this time flat on his back, and Ash snuggled into his side, one arm tucked under her and one slung over his chest. A smile pulled at the corners of her mouth, and she let it stay as long as it wanted.

Because though this day had started with worry and uncertainty, it was going to end in the most wonderful way.

The show went on and on, and Ash felt sure it would end soon. Burke shifted, and Ash lifted up to see his face. "Okay?"

He turned then, his broad back shielding her from Leo—and the fireworks. "I'm dying for the do-over," he whispered, his lips trailing from her temple down her cheek. "What do you think?"

Oh, she wanted to kiss him under these fireworks, but

she hesitated. It was dark, sure, but with every explosion, the sky lit up. Anyone could see them.

Ash decided she didn't care. She wanted this to be her one moment for today, so she tilted her head in just the right way and caught the corner of his mouth with hers.

She aligned their lips, and she didn't just hold hers against his. She kissed him, the fireworks now exploding in her stomach, her chest, her entire body.

Because *this* was a kiss—and it was so much better than the first. In fact, the passion Burke poured into it exceeded even her most wild fantasies.

She matched his movement, hoping he could feel her desire for him too, revealing how she felt about him and not caring.

He broke the connection, said, "Ash," and promptly kissed her again.

Chapter Eleven

A *sh, Ash, Ash.*
Her name echoed in his head as he kissed her.
True, he had not kissed a woman in quite a long time. And the first time had been a complete disaster. But Burke seemed to have remembered what to do, where to put his hands, how to move his mouth, to make this kiss one of the most memorable he'd ever had.

Somewhere beyond him and Ash, the music ended and a cheer went up. He knew enough to pull away then, because the floodlights would switch on at any moment. The last thing he needed was to be caught by Leo—by anyone—kissing Ash.

She rested her forehead against his collarbone, and he wondered if she could feel the rapid-fire beat of his pulse. He didn't care if she could. He'd said it all with the kiss anyway—and he *liked* Ash.

They breathed in together, something they'd

perfected while they ran down the beach, and Burke really liked this version a whole lot better. Around them, people moved even in the dark, but he held very still, holding her close for as long as he dared.

He moved, and she slipped easily away from him, the white lights flooding the beach a few moments later. He stood and collected the blanket, as well as Ash's empty popcorn container.

She helped her niece and nephew clean up their blankets, picked up trash on the beach, and shouldered her purse. After slipping her feet into her flip flops, she put her hand in his and they made their way through the garden gate along with everyone else.

Somehow Leo and Genevieve got separated from them, and Burke didn't see his parents either. It was all fine. It meant he didn't have to worry about anyone watching him, trying to work out if he was being genuine with Ash or not.

He was.

He liked her. The adrenaline and excitement still racing through him proved that. He simply wasn't sure how far he was willing to take things. His dad wanted an engagement. A ring on her finger. An heir.

But his feelings for Ash were very, very new. Could he take the time he needed to make sure the relationship was right for both of them? Or would his father demand a diamond sooner rather than later?

Burke wished he didn't worry so much about things. But the non-worrying genes seemed to have gone to

Kayla and Krista, who approached him as he and Ash entered the parking lot.

"There you are," Kayla said. "I didn't see you all night."

"Not hard to find," he said. "We barely moved on the beach." He glanced at Ash. "You guys know Ash."

Krista, just as blonde as Burke and almost identical to Kayla except for her slightly more upturned nose, turned to Ash and said, "Of course." She hugged Ash and added, "I think it's sweet you two are finally together."

"Finally?" Burke asked at the same time Kayla said, "We thought for a while you guys would get together, and then you never did." She shrugged and looked at her twin.

"But you are now." Krista beamed at them like she'd personally set Burke up with Ash. He had no idea why his sisters were acting so weird.

"What's going on?" he asked.

"Nothing," Kayla said innocently, which raised all kinds of red flags in Burke's mind.

"Right," he said. "I don't believe you."

"Dad said you're engaged," Krista said.

"But we know you just started dating," Kayla said.

"Not months ago," Krista added.

"We would've known." Kayla nodded, glancing back and forth between Burke and Ash. Every word they said sent more ice into Burke's bloodstream.

"It's none of your business," Burke said, digging in his shorts pocket for his keys.

"I mean, we know you go over to her place a lot." Krista exchanged a glance with Kayla, and they did that strange twin non-verbal communication he hated.

"You do?" Ash asked.

"Yeah, sure." Kayla said, this tag-teaming getting extremely boring. And annoying. "I mean, he tries to act like he's out all night partying, but he's really just at your place."

"So maybe you have been dating longer than we thought." Krista looked at them, her bright blue eyes harboring hope.

"No," Ash said, when Burke wished she wouldn't say anything. He'd have to teach her how to deal with his sisters. Engaging with them never helped. "It's new."

"Ha." Kayla nudged her sister. "How new?"

"This interrogation is over," Burke said, finally getting his keys out and unlocking the car. "Come on, Ash. You don't have to answer their questions."

"Just give me something," Krista said. "I need a new pair of shoes. There's these cute wedges at Sandoval's."

Ash paused as she went around the front of the car. "Do you have a bet on this or something?"

"Just with each other," the twins said together, which caused Burke to roll his eyes.

"Ash," he said. "Don't."

"Seventy-nine days," Ash said, and she continued to her door and got in.

Burke closed the door behind her and glared at

Krista and Kayla as he came back to the driver's side door. "You two are impossible."

"You really like her," Krista said, cocking her head and making her ponytail swing.

"Of course I do," Burke said. "What do you think this is?" He would never, ever tell anyone that the relationship had started under false pretenses. No one needed to know that. And it wasn't seventy-nine days ago anyway.

He pulled open the door and got behind the wheel, effectively shutting out his sisters. "Sorry about that," he said.

"Oh, they're harmless." Ash had already buckled her seatbelt. "Leo seemed to back off pretty easily too."

"Yeah." Burke wondered what that was about and if he'd have to deal with Leo on his own later. Probably. "Just back to your place?"

"Yes, please. I have a meeting in the morning with an out-of-town bride. They have a plane to catch, so it's at eight o'clock."

"Wow," he said. "That's terrible."

She laughed. "Oh, please. You'll be sitting on your bench by four a.m."

He chuckled and couldn't deny it. "Probably, yeah."

"No probably about it," Ash said, reaching over and taking his hand in hers. "That was a much better kiss, by the way."

Burke burst into laughter, glad when Ash's higher

pitched giggles joined in. "I'm glad. I was worried I'd forgotten how there for a while."

She made a happy little sigh and snuggled into the seat while he drove her home. He pulled up to her house, something he'd done countless times before. "What was with the seventy-nine days?" he asked.

She turned toward him, her eyes like magnets pulling at him, urging him closer. "That's how long I've had my little crush."

Burke absorbed the statement. "I don't think it's a crush anymore, Ash," he said, the power behind his words soft and fragile.

A smile crossed her face, enhancing her beauty and making him grin too. "No, probably not."

He leaned over the console, and she met him halfway, and Burke shared another kiss with her he wouldn't soon forget.

———

BURKE RODE THE FOURTH OF JULY HIGH FOR DAYS. EVEN getting up in the morning was easier. Breathing was easier. Everything was easier with Ash in his life.

Then he'd stop and pause, realizing that Ash had always been in his life, and that it was something else making his smile appear so readily and the sun seem so bright.

Probably the fact that you get to kiss her, he thought as he stretched out his right calf. The leg had been bothering him lately, and he'd been paying extra attention to it during his warm up and cool down.

Ash was late, and Burke turned toward the stretch of sand where she always appeared. "Where is she, Dolly?" Today, the golden retriever had already flopped in the sand, her tongue out like she'd already run around the bay.

His phone chimed, and he unzipped his pocket to retrieve it. Won't make it. Something's come up with my mom.

Alarm sang through Burke. His first thought was to skip his own morning run and go find out how he could help Ash. That was a very boyfriendly thing to do, right?

And exactly what he would've done for Bridgette. "Maybe that was what had tied her down," he muttered. He gripped his phone too tight, hating that he was second-guessing everything about his behavior now.

What would he have done a month ago if he'd gotten this same text? His brain hurt, because it was hard to think through a situation that didn't exist, especially when it was colored with new feelings and unknown expectations.

He thought of that notebook she'd first written in. The agreement she'd wanted to make when their relationship was fake. He really wished he had one now, some sort of code he knew to follow.

He touched the phone icon near her name at the top of the text and lifted his device to his ear as the line rang.

"Burke?" she answered, a definite note of surprise in her voice.

"Do you need any help?" he asked, bypassing the typical greeting. "With your mom. I can skip running this morning."

"No, it's fine." She sounded annoyed, and a car horn honked, filling the line. Burke pulled the phone away from his ear for a moment.

"Ash," he said. "Are you lying to me?" It was much harder to tell on the phone, without being able to see her eyes.

"No," she said. "I'm just in this early-morning traffic, and I don't really know what's wrong with Mom. I just had a feeling I should call her this morning, and she didn't answer. So I'm going to go check on her."

"So you'll call me once you know."

"Sure," she said.

"All right." Burke normally would've hung up, stretched his legs again, and started down the beach with just Dolly. But he stayed on the line for another moment, long enough for Ash to say, "Come *on*. The light is green."

He chuckled and said, "Talk to you later," before hanging up. He then stretched, ran, and returned to his condo to shower before he returned to the flower farm. He'd already gone through the morning routine with his father, but he went into his dad's office when he arrived back at the building anyway.

"Morning, Dad."

"Burke, there you are," he said, rising as if he'd been looking all over for Burke. As if he didn't know Burke went running every single morning, and on which beaches. Of course he knew all of that.

"Here I am."

"Our website guy had a great idea." He clapped Burke on the shoulder as he passed him. "Come with me."

Burke had spent a fair bit of time with the public relations department, which employed a couple of publicists, writers, and a man who kept their website running and up-to-date. Computers didn't interest Burke all that much, unless there was a particularly addicting video game. Even then, he usually only played for a few hours before getting bored.

"Matai," his dad said upon arriving in the man's office. "Here he is."

"Good, good," the shorter man said in an accented voice. "Let me get Linnie."

"Linnie?" Burke asked, twisting as the man rushed past him and out of his office. "Dad? What's going on?"

"They're going to do a story on your engagement. For the website." He beamed at Burke like this was the best possible news on the planet. But Burke's blood turned to ice, and he sucked in a breath as if he'd just been doused with similarly cold water.

"Dad, I don't think that's a good idea."

"Why not?" Some of the happiness left his father's face, and in its place, suspicion mingled with confusion.

"It's just that Ash is really private," Burke said. "It's not like the whole island doesn't already know about us." As he spoke, Burke realized how true he'd spoken. Sure, there were a lot of tourists in Getaway Bay, but the locals on the island were a pretty tight-knit group. And word did spread like wildfire sometimes.

"This is more than the island," his dad said. "This is an announcement of my retirement and how I'm passing the operation onto you on January first."

"Dad." Burke couldn't say much more than that. There was so much wrong with what was happening. He wasn't even sure how much he liked Ash. He wanted to go slow and make sure he was being his authentic self and not who he thought she wanted him to be. And getting married by the end of the year?

Yeah, that wasn't going to happen.

"Have you bought her a ring yet?" His dad pressed his lips together as Matai and Linnie entered the office.

Burke shook his head, knowing he needed to explain further, but not wanting to do it in front of their chief writer and website developer.

His father turned to Matai. "I'm sorry, we've had something come up. Can we come back later today?"

"Sure, sure," Matai said, and Burke's father led the way out of the office. He left a heavy wake of electricity behind him, and Burke simply walked through it.

As soon as the elevator doors sealed them into some semblance of privacy, Burke said, "Dad, I just don't think

Ash and I will be married by then. We're taking things slow."

His dad snorted. "You started dating a few months ago and you're already engaged."

"Sort of," Burke hedged. "No ring, remember?" He should just tell him the whole truth—that he and Ash had literally started dating a few days ago. *Days.* That he'd fibbed earlier so his father wouldn't consider giving the farm to Krista or Kayla.

The elevator doors opened before Burke could say anything, and both of his sisters stood there with armfuls of flowers. "Happy anniversary, Daddy," they said together, saving Burke from having to explain further.

Chapter Twelve

Ash climbed the front steps to her childhood home, noting the way the rain gutter had separated from the roof. It dipped in a strange way, and she made a mental note to call Leo about it. He could come fix it, or he'd at least know who to call to come fix it.

She knocked and eased open the door. "Mom?" The interior of the house was still pretty dark, though the glorious Hawaiian sun had started to rise and paint the island in gold morning light.

The scent of burnt coffee met her nose, but she couldn't decide if it was from this morning or yesterday. "Mom?" she called again.

A noise thunked from the back of the house, and Ash thought for a moment she should take something with her. Maybe an animal had gotten in the house or something. She liked dogs and cats just fine, but anything more than that, and she'd rather be armed.

Unfortunately, her mother's living room was void of weapons or tools. So Ash called, "Mom?" for the third time and went around the corner into the kitchen. The coffee was definitely from this morning, as the red light on the maker was shining brightly. A mug sat on the counter beside it, along with the sugar bowl, but her mom was not there.

Ash switched off the coffee maker and moved around the corner again and into the mud room, walking quickly now. Sometimes her mom liked to go outside in the early morning hours before it got too hot. The yard didn't look nearly as good as it once had, but she did the best she could, and it made her happy.

Leo had suggested a gardening service once, and their mother had gotten upset. Said, "You can't take everything away from me just because I'm sick."

So Ash and Leo had let her keep doing the yard work.

Another thunk sounded as Ash pushed through the back door, and then another as her mom tossed another red potato into a bucket. "There you are," Ash said, putting a smile on her face.

Her mom glanced up, the color of her face impossible for Ash to determine under the wide brim of her sun hat. "Oh, I missed your call, didn't I?"

"It's okay, Mom." Ash moved out into the sunlight and approached the garden. "How are the potatoes?"

"These are a bit small." Her mom looked down at the ground and sighed as if a poor red potato crop was the worst thing to happen to her. As Ash got closer, she could see her mom looked good today, with good color in her face.

Ash wrapped her arms around her mom and gave her a tight hug. Her mom patted her on the back with her dirty gardening gloves and said, "You okay, Ashy?"

She wasn't sure why she felt like someone had poured gelatin inside her whole body. But she trembled and quaked as if they had. "Yeah, I'm okay."

"Your wedding was last week, wasn't it?"

If only, Ash thought, though she knew what her mom was referencing. "Yes, one done. Another one in a week, but that dress has been done for a while." She needed to get over to Your Tidal Forever today to pick up a couple of new contracts and set up meetings with Charlotte and the brides. Apparently a pair of sisters had gotten engaged to a set of twins, and they wanted a double wedding.

Ash was happy for the business. It kept her busy and kept her bills paid. But she was starting to wonder what really brought her happiness, and if she could find it with a needle and thread.

"Are you seeing anyone?" her mom asked next, stepping back and bending over to extract another potato from the dirt.

It was an innocent question, Ash knew. She'd talked about her boyfriends freely in the past. Yet, for some reason, she'd never told her mom about her crush on

Burke, nor the fact that they'd started a fake relationship that had become real in the past three weeks.

"I'm actually seeing Burke." Ash bit her lip so her smile wouldn't spread so quickly.

"What?" Her mother straightened and looked at Ash like she'd just said she'd grown wings. "Burke Lawson? The man you run with?"

"Yes, him." Ash shrugged. "He's…handsome. Employed. Going to take over his father's business one day. I like him."

Her mother blinked at her. "What does Leo say?"

"Leo has his own life to deal with," Ash said, maybe with a bit too much bite. The fact that her mother knew Leo hadn't approved of a teenage relationship between Burke and Ash made her teeth grind.

"Besides, I'm thirty-five-years-old, and not getting any younger, and I'd like to make my own wedding dress one day."

"Oh, honey. You will." Her mom wrapped her arms around Ash again, her presence comforting and sure.

Ash didn't want to say that she hoped her mom would be there. She'd only cause guilt for her mother and disappointment in herself. After all, the truth was, there was a very real possibility the cancer would take her mom before Ash got a chance to walk down the aisle. Just like the ocean had taken her father.

She drew in a deep breath, stepped back, and looked out over the valley. The trees were so green, the flowers so bright, and the water so perfectly blue. A sense of contentment filled her, even though her left hand didn't bear a diamond.

"I love this island," she said. "And this thing with Burke is very new. We're going slow, so it's possible nothing will come of it." But when she thought about their last couple of kisses, she wanted to stomp on the accelerator. She'd always suspected he knew how to kiss a woman, but after that awful first encounter, she'd formed some doubts.

Doubts he'd eradicated swiftly.

"Well, now that I know you're okay, I better get in to work," Ash said. "How does take-out sound tonight?" Her mother didn't normally like eating anything from a restaurant, claiming they used chemicals and other things that made her cancer grow faster. But every once in a while, Ash could bring up sushi or a ramen bowl from her mother's favorite Japanese restaurant.

"Sounds great, honey. Whatever is easiest for you." She gave her another smile and reached for another potato.

Ash left her mom in the garden and headed back down the hill into town. She passed the turnoff for Petals & Leis and remembered she needed to call Burke. She would once she got settled at work. He was probably still running down the sand anyway.

She showered, dressed, and drove over to her tiny shop in a strip of other tiny shops. She'd no sooner sat down in her chair and pulled her calendar out of her bag when the bells on the front door rang.

Ash stood and moved to the doorway, her heels clicking against the floor. "Oh, Zara." Ash's smile was genuine and felt warm on her face. She embraced her friend and said, "What are you doing here?"

Zara tucked her dark hair and said, "My sister is getting married, and she wants non-traditional brides-maid's dresses."

Alarm tugged through Ash. "What does your mom say about that?" Zara's family was Indian, and quite traditional. "Anaya isn't going to wear a saree at all?"

"She says she will for the party." Zara followed Ash back into her office. "But she wants more of a western ceremony. I told her I'd talk to you about bridesmaid dresses."

Ash pulled out her notebook and placed it next to her calendar. She opened a drawer as she said, "I have a questionnaire for brides. I mean, I know you're not the bride, but this helps me know what they like, what they're thinking, and when they need it."

"No, I'm not the bride." Zara looked down at the packet of papers Ash handed to her. "Seems I never am, am I?"

Their eyes met, and keen understanding flowed between them. "I've made over four hundred custom wedding dresses in my lifetime," Ash finally said. "One day, I really hope I get to make my own."

"At least you have a boyfriend," Zara said, misery in every syllable. "And a small family so not every single sister who gets married is a reminder that you can't even get a date."

Ash covered Zara's hand with hers. "I know a guy who might go out with you."

"Yeah, who?"

"Have you ever thought about taking scuba diving lessons?"

"Ryan Bonnett?" Zara asked immediately. "No, thanks. That guy gives me the creeps."

Ash burst out laughing, and Zara joined her. "No, for now, I just need six bridesmaid's dresses. Anaya said blue or purple."

An hour later, Zara left the shop, having ordered six dresses for the following April. At least Ash would have time to work on them amidst all her other projects. When she realized what time it was, she swiped her purse off her desk and headed for the door.

A shadow passed in front of her, but she couldn't stop herself in time and she crashed into the man who entered her shop at the same time she tried to leave it.

"Oh!" Her hands scrambled for something to grab onto, otherwise she was going to fall backward. And in her tight skirt and heels, that was not a sight she wanted anyone to see.

"Hey, hey." Burke's voice entered her ears, and his arms went around her, steadying her. "I got you."

She found her balance and looked up into his handsome face. "What are you doing here?" Her voice was breathy and weak, her pulse hammering out of control.

"You never called. I thought I'd come by and see what was going on this morning."

"Mm." Ash closed her eyes and stretched up a few inches to kiss Burke. He received her willingly, and Ash's body felt soft while her mind catalogued every movement of his mouth, every spicy scent of his cologne, the hint of flowers beneath that, and the way his hands slid down her back and returned to her hair.

She finally broke their kiss and whispered, "She was fine. Just out in the garden and missed my call."

He swayed, taking her with him, and she remembered where she needed to go. "I have a meeting at Your Tidal Forever in fifteen minutes."

"So we can't go to lunch?"

"When I'm finished we can." She beamed up at him, glad when she saw the softness in his eyes. It looked like adoration, and she was finally convinced that his feelings for her weren't out of pity or because she'd said she liked him first.

"When will you be finished?"

"I have no idea. I'm meeting with two brides. Sisters."

"Could be hours." A playful glint entered his eyes.

"Could be." She laughed and moved out of his arms. "You can wait here, or I'll text you when I'm done." She tried to step around him, but he blocked her path one more time.

"This is okay, right?"

"What is?" She didn't like the vulnerability in his eyes. The questions. The anxiety.

"Me showing up here, wanting to go to lunch."

"Of course it is." She cocked her head. "Why wouldn't it be?"

He shrugged, though Ash had a very strong feeling that he knew exactly why he was asking. "Can we talk about it at lunch?"

"Sure." He moved out of the way, and then followed her out. "I'll head back to the farm. Just text me when you're ready."

She slipped her hand in his as they walked into the parking lot, and he gripped her fingers when she started to pull away at her car.

"What do you think about going to get a ring tonight?" He didn't look at her when he asked, and that annoyed Ash as much as the ruse of their engagement.

"You think we need to?" She'd been hoping that part of the agreement would just disappear, that he wouldn't press the issue unless his father did.

Which meant his father had.

"At least for my parents." He cupped her face in both of his hands, shooting fire into her jaw and down her neck. "My dad, really."

Ash's throat felt tight, so she just nodded. He kissed her quickly and said, "All right. Go to your meeting," with a playful smile.

She did, but now her mind wasn't as focused on the

sisters, but on why Burke couldn't just tell his dad they weren't really engaged.

It doesn't matter, she told herself as she navigated the streets over to the east bay and down to the wedding planning building. She and Burke *were* dating, and he genuinely seemed to like her.

Didn't he?

Chapter Thirteen

B urke didn't want to go back to Petals & Leis, but somehow his truck took him up to the flower farm anyway. He sat in the air conditioning, unwilling to get out and go work in the fields. What he wanted to do was head home, pull on a wet suit, and go surfing.

But Ash's meeting could last an hour or four, and he wanted to be able to take her to lunch when she finished.

He made a quick decision and sent Ash a text. *I'm going to go surfing. My regular spot. Rain check on lunch?*

He'd put the truck in reverse to back out of the spot when a message came back. Sure. Call you later. Headed in to my meeting now.

Half an hour later, Burke stood in the sand, the heat of it almost burning his bare feet. He relished the feel of it, as it made him feel like he was exactly where he should be. The waves weren't particularly impressive today, as it was nearly noon and the tide came in much earlier.

He didn't care. He'd left his surf board at home, actually, and brought his body board instead. The waves came in and went out, and he finally found one he wanted to hit. Flipping the board out into the water, he ran after it and jumped on, riding the board out to the wave and cresting it.

He rode down the wave before finally stepping off in shallow water, the cooler water against his skin in direct contrast with the super-heated July sun. He'd left the wet suit at home, the water temperature definitely warm enough without it.

The waves soothed him, and he played with them for an hour before his stomach roared and demanded food. He could still lunch with Ash, he reasoned, so he ran up the beach to Manni's, the best taco stand on the sand.

The line was always long, but mid-week, and an hour past lunchtime, he didn't have to wait too long. He accepted his tacos from DJ, a guy about his age who'd taken the mobile home and converted it into a restaurant that put out the best fish tacos on the island.

"Saw you riding the waves," he said, like he had time to talk. "Maybe tomorrow, we can go in the morning?" The similarly blond-haired, blue-eyed man looked at Burke expectantly.

"Yeah, sure," Burke said. "Early? Like five-thirty."

DJ grinned and collected another taco for the next customer. "See you out there."

Burke wandered away from the taco stand, eating

through his three shrimp tacos before even leaving the shade of the palm trees.

He sank into the sand on the cusp of where sun met shade and watched the people on the beach. This was the less busy side of the double half-moon bays, but there were still plenty of people. Families, couples, children, dogs.

Burke basked in the vibrant atmosphere of it all, the roar of the waves faint and in the distance, but still loud enough to soothe his soul. And for the first time in a long time, he didn't feel stuck.

Bridgette had cemented him in place, and he thought through the last six years and what he'd done. Not much. Got through each day. Pretended.

And he was really tired of pretending—which was why he did not want to go buy an engagement ring with Ash that night. Not if it wasn't going to be real. She'd seemed surprised when he'd asked too, but he didn't know how to satisfy his father and make Ash happy.

He picked up his board, dodged through the people and blankets and umbrellas, and went back to the shoreline to give his concerns to the ocean. It had always taken them from him before, and by the time he pulled himself out of the surf for the last time, Ash stood on the beach in her tight skirt and pale blue blouse.

She shielded her eyes with her hand and searched the water. Burke flipped his hair out of his face and stayed low in the water, watching her. Trying to figure out how he truly felt.

Ash was smart, driven, loyal, and kind. He'd never had a problem laughing with her, and they did talk about most things. All things, now that he'd told her about Bridgette. She hadn't judged him, or asked him why he'd kept proposing to a woman who clearly didn't want him.

He stood and waved, calling, "Ash," to get her attention. She found him and waved, a smile on her face. He slopped through the water to the wet sand, bending to pick up his body board as it rode the waves in and out.

"All done?" he asked as he approached.

Her eyes lingered on his torso before migrating to his. "Yeah, all done."

"Feel like tacos or something that requires me to put on a shirt?"

"We can get a drink at The Straw and maybe head over to Sweet Breeze?" she asked. "I'm dying for some of their sliders, and my mom wants a ramen bowl from the restaurant on the fourth floor."

"Sounds great." He tucked his board under one arm and took her hand with his free one. "Tell me about the meeting."

"You don't really care," she said as they stepped past the other groups on the beach.

"Sure I do." Burke glanced at her out of the corner of his eye. "I always ask you about your clients."

"Yeah, I guess."

He took an extra-large step and moved in front of her. "What's going on?"

"It's just...." She sighed, and without her sunglasses

to hide behind, he saw the indecision racing through her eyes.

"What, Ash?" He wanted to tip her head up to look into his eyes. Kiss her right there on the beach. But there were too many people watching, and he had some decency.

"I'm just hungry." She started walking again, putting her hand squarely in his this time, and added, "The sisters are interesting. They're from the ranch, and they're marrying twins. They want wildly different things though. Different dresses, different cakes. Basically all they're doing together is the ceremony. Charlotte looked like she was going to blow a gasket." Ash trilled out a laugh, and Burke squeezed her hand.

He once again thought about how this conversation would've been different a month ago. She probably would've said all the same things. Laughed the same way. But his heart rate wouldn't have accelerated and he, of course, wouldn't have been holding her hand.

"Ash," he said as they got in line at The Straw. "I was feeling bad about asking you for this favor, but now that I'm thinking about it, I'm glad I did."

"Oh, yeah?" She lifted her eyebrows in challenge. "And why's that?"

He lifted her hand to his lips and kissed her wrist. "Because if I hadn't, you would've never told me about your crush, and we wouldn't be here, doing this." He gazed at her, hoping his true meaning had come through in his words.

She gave him a closed-mouth smile and moved up in line. His chest squeezed. He'd said something wrong. And Burke suddenly hated talking. He liked it when things were light, and she was telling him about her clients or he told her about the clematis that had bloomed last week.

But all this conversation about his feelings? Yeah, he didn't like disclosing that stuff. He always did it wrong.

Maybe that was how you messed things up with Bridgette too, he thought as Ash tipped onto her toes and put in her order. She paid before Burke could get his thoughts to align, leaving him to order and pay for his separately.

Desperation and frustration dove through him, the same way he'd been diving head-first into the waves this afternoon. Ash had let go of his hand at some point, and she made no effort to touch him again, or even talk to him.

"Thanks, Sasha," she said to the woman as she leaned out of the stand and handed Ash her drink. Sasha's eyes cut between Ash and Burke, and he simply looked back. It was like the sun had fried his brain.

He got his drink from a Polynesian woman and he and Ash set off down the beachwalk that led through the jungle over to the other bay. Though there was plenty of noise around them, the silence between them felt suffocating and he could barely sip his smoothie.

About halfway to Sweet Breeze, he said, "I'm sorry, Ash. What did I say?"

"Do you really like me?" She stopped right in the middle of the beachwalk, causing the other pedestrians to flow around her.

"What? Of course I do." Burke glanced at an older couple who had obviously overheard them.

"And not just because I like you." She edged out of the way a little bit so people could get by.

Burke stepped off the beachwalk altogether, the soft-packed sand beside the boards shifting a little with his weight. "I mean, maybe a thing with you wasn't on my radar before, but—"

"A thing with me." She cocked her hip and sipped her drink. Her dark eyes flashed with anger, and Burke felt himself digging deeper and deeper.

"A relationship," he clarified. "I guess I wasn't looking at you. You're my best friend."

"Great, so I was overlooked." She rolled her eyes and started walking again. The way she kept starting and stopping at random times had him completely discombobulated. His smoothie sloshed over the rim as he tried to catch up to her.

"Ash," he said, catching her after a few strides. "It's not that. You've always had someone else. A boyfriend. Some guy you're trying to get to ask you out. Something."

She didn't look at him, but at this rate, they'd reach Sweet Breeze in a matter of minutes. "So you're saying because I've been unavailable you haven't seen me."

"Ash." He stepped in front of her this time, creating

another roadblock. He didn't care. He looked down at her, desperate for her to understand. "I haven't been seeing *anyone* for six years."

There was more to say, but he couldn't find the words. Somehow, he felt like he'd said them all. Understanding flowed through her beautiful eyes, and Burke couldn't believe this woman—this beautiful, forgiving woman—had been in front of him all this time and he hadn't *seen* her.

"Okay?" He swallowed, his throat dry. He took a sip of his smoothie, the tart raspberries combining with the tangy orange. "So maybe I'm out of practice with talking about stuff. Maybe I get a do-over, like with the kiss."

"Maybe," she said, nudging him out of her way with her palm. "I just don't want to invest much in this if it's a joke to you."

"It's not a joke."

"If you don't really like me."

"I really like you."

"If it's just a show for your dad."

"It's not just a show." Well, it had started that way, but things had changed for Burke quite rapidly.

Ash paused one more time and smiled up at him. "Great. Because my mother would like you to come with me to take her dinner tonight." She patted his chest a couple of times. "And you know you can't get anything by a kindergarten teacher. They see and know everything." Ash got a few paces ahead of him while Burke started to sweat over meeting her mother.

Of course, he'd met her mother plenty of times. As Burke-the-best-friend. Not Burke-the-man-who's-currently-kissing-your-daughter.

"She hasn't taught for years," he called after Ash, who only tipped her head back and laughed.

Chapter Fourteen

Ash's chest continued to pinch through her late lunch with Burke. But at least the tension in the very air around them had dissipated. Still, she didn't like how she had to work so hard to convince herself that he liked her. Did it matter what the reasons were? Or when the attraction had begun?

"How's your mom doing?" he asked as the waiter brought their check.

"She looked really good this morning, actually." Ash saw the golden sun haloing her mother in her mind's eye. "She loves to work in the garden."

"I'm surprised she still does it."

"If it's been several days since her treatment, it's usually okay."

"When's her next one?"

"Friday." Four more days. These were usually the best

days of the month for her mother—and for Ash too. "Should we go get her ramen bowl?"

"Sure." He picked up the check and threw down some cash before they left. Their walk back over to the other bay so he could collect his board and she could get back to her office was easy, leisurely. The afternoon crowds on the beach had started to thin as locals took their kids home for dinner and tourists concluded their day under the sun so they could get ready to enjoy the nightlife in Getaway Bay.

"Want to shower and meet me at my place?" she asked as he picked up his board from where he'd leaned it against the Manni's building.

"Sure." He met her eye and glanced around, sweeping one arm around her and pulling her further behind the mobile home that now served tacos and burritos.

"Burke." She giggled and kept a tight grip on the plastic bag containing her mother's soup.

"I just want to kiss you," he murmured. "So you'll know."

"Know what?"

He answered with a slow, heated touch of his mouth to hers. "How I feel," he said, his breath drifting along her chin. He kissed her again, and Ash felt the last whispers of her doubt melt away.

By the time he pulled away, the temperature in the shade had doubled, and Ash's heart felt like it was about to burst.

"All right?" He tucked her hair behind her ear and watched her.

She kept her head ducked for another few seconds, tasting him on her lips and enjoying this sensation of being liked.

Sure, other men had kissed her, but Milo had never kissed her like this. Not even once. Not even the first time.

Burke didn't want to own Ash. No, his touch testified that he cherished her. She looked up and met his eyes. "All right."

He smiled a soft, lazy smile that she rarely saw as he only pulled it out when he was alone with her. "So does take-out with your mom require formal clothing? Or can I wear shorts?"

"Whatever's fine. I'm wearing this unless you take really long showers." Which she knew he didn't.

They separated after that, and she walked the last half-mile to her cottage alone. Her grass looked a little on the dry side, so she set the sprinklers to run before dashing inside with the ramen so she could at least tame her hair back into submission.

The wind off the bay always tied her curls in knots, and she worked them out as quickly as she could. She'd just stepped into her closet to change when she heard Burke call, "I'm coming in."

"I'm changing! Be out in a sec." Ash pulled off her work clothes and slipped into a pair of shorts and a sleeveless shirt the color of pumpkins. Her mother had bought it for her for Christmas last year and would appreciate seeing it. Ash tried to get the ribbing to lay flat, but she'd need an iron to do that, and she didn't have time.

After touching up her makeup, she found Burke in the kitchen, standing in front of the open fridge, peering in. "We just ate," she said.

"And walked like a mile," he said, glancing at her. "Wow, you look great."

He did too, wearing gray slacks and a bright blue polo. "Those are not shorts," she said.

"It's your mom," he replied, abandoning the fridge and coming toward her with a slightly predatory look on his face.

"I just redid my lipstick," she said, holding up her hand. "The kissing has to wait."

"Wait?" Burke's face scrunched up like he didn't know what that word meant.

Ash cocked her head and grinned at him. "Come on. Mom eats early." Ash didn't mention that her mother would be asleep by seven p.m., especially as she'd found her in the garden so early this morning.

But then there'd be plenty of time for kissing after that. She gave Burke a smile she hoped conveyed all the things she was thinking and reached for his hand. They chatted about this and that as he drove her up the hill to her mother's house.

He was easy to be with. Fun to talk to. Ash laughed at

something he said as they mounted the steps and she opened the front door. "Mom, we're here."

"Come in," she called from further in the house, and Ash exchanged a final glance with Burke before leading him toward the kitchen. She lifted the bag containing her mother's ramen bowl onto the counter just as her mother pulled a tray of sweet buns out of the oven.

"Mom, I told you I was bringing dinner."

"I know. There's nothing better with ramen than fresh bread." Her mom smiled at her, and Ash immediately saw the exhaustion in her eyes. Dark eyes like Ash's. Of course, her father had had dark eyes too, but Ash liked to think hers twinkled like her mother's when she laughed.

"Mom, you didn't need to bake."

"I had nothing else to do this afternoon," she said, slipping the oven mitts off and looking past Ash to Burke. "Hello, Burke. My, don't you look handsome and so grown up." She hugged him like they were old friends and reached into the plastic bag to take out her soup.

Burke filled his plate with bread and joined them at the table, where her mother proceeded to dip a corner of her bun into her soup. "So, Burke. How are your parents?"

"Just fine, Mrs. Fox. Well, my mother was sick for a week or two last month, but she seems to be doing better."

"That's good." Her mom smiled, and Ash took a bun

from Burke's plate, the nerves in her stomach demanding she quell them with carbs.

"Yeah, my father is drawing up papers to turn Petals and Leis over to me on January first."

Ash swung her attention to him. "Really?"

"Yeah. Didn't I tell you?" His blue eyes danced as he reached for the butter and added a healthy amount to his roll.

"That's great," Ash's mother said. "That farm has been in your family for such a long time."

"Yes," Burke said, all formal and proper. Ash glanced at him again, a giggle forming in her throat. She pushed it down with another bite of bread.

"I hope one of my children will keep this house." Her mom's gaze landed on Ash, and Ash felt like someone had sucked all the oxygen out of the air.

"Mom." She reached across the table and covered her mom's hand with both of hers. "Leo said you willed it to him."

"But he's just built that big place on the bluff. What with his new technology something-or-other being sold for so much." She pulled her hand away and waved it. "He won't want this place. And you love your cottage on the beach. And Davis won't come back to the island."

Her mother saddened at that, and Ash did too. She hadn't thought of her younger brother in a while. He'd had a falling out with their father a decade ago, left Getaway Bay, and never been back. Not even for the funeral.

Ash had tried to find out from Leo what the disagreement was about, but her older brother didn't know. Or at least he acted like he didn't.

"Why'd Davis leave?" Ash asked her mom.

"He...." She looked up and met Ash's eye. "Something happened. If he wouldn't come back for the funeral, he won't come back to this house after I die."

"Mom."

"So," she said loudly. "Burke. Tell me about yourself. What have you been up to the last twenty years?"

———

A WEEK PASSED. THEN TWO. JULY MELTED—LITERALLY melted—into August, and Ash enjoyed every slow summer night with Burke she could get. Sometimes they laid on the beach in each other's arms. Sometimes he drove her around the island until they found a good vantage point to watch the sun set. Sometimes they went to restaurants and movies and up into his flower fields.

She liked those field trips the best, as Burke became a different man among the rows and rows of carnations, or out under the branches of the plumeria trees. He was born to run that farm, and though she'd never run into his father on their evening jaunts around the flower fields, she'd recommitted herself to making sure Burke got his inheritance.

They hadn't talked about the fake engagement again. Nor had they gone to pick out a ring. She didn't want to continue a false relationship with him; she was quite happy with the real one she and Burke were currently experiencing.

She sat at the sewing machine one morning, the needle flying along the pale blue satin to get the straps on before Zara and her sisters showed up. It had only been a month, but she'd managed to get the other four dresses ready for fittings. She just had this one left.

And thirty minutes before they all showed up.

So she sewed, and unpicked a seam that didn't lay right, trying again with the delicate fabric. She'd just pulled it out of the machine and clipped a thread when the bell on her front door rang.

Feminine chatter sounded, and someone laughed as Ash moved to greet them. She grinned at Zara, who led the women into the shop. They all had dark skin like hers, their Indian heritage bringing with it stunning beauty and deep, almost black eyes.

"Hi, Zara." Ash embraced her friend, feeling the tension in her shoulders. "I've got all the dresses ready for you ladies." She stepped back, her purely professional face in position. She flashed Zara a quick smile first and turned back to the other women.

"Who wants to go first?"

"I will."

"Abish, right?" Ash asked, sure she'd butchered the name.

"She goes by Abi," Zara said. "Second oldest. Married to Bill Henney."

"Oh, right. Of course." Ash had not made any of the dresses for the Reddy sisters, as they'd all had a traditional Indian wedding. She'd attended the last one with Zara, her rented saree one of the most beautiful pieces of clothing she'd ever worn. She'd thought about sewing one for herself, but in the end, she hadn't had time.

She helped Abi into the dressing room while the other women migrated toward the lemon water and cookies Ash had set out for this fitting. She worked for the next hour and a half, never happier that she'd learned to turn down the air conditioning during a fitting. That extra three degrees helped keep everyone cool, including her, as they went in and out of the dressing room, made notes and pinned fabric into place.

One by one, all the sisters got their dress fitting, until only Zara remained. She was the slimmest of the sisters, and her dress shone like the morning sky against her skin. "It's not bad," Ash said.

"Are you kidding?" Zara cupped her hands over her chest. "This has to be taken *way* in."

Ash made the adjustment, wrote down the notes she needed, and glanced at the tray to see there were two cookies left. Thank goodness. She'd earned them, and she really wanted to stuff them both in her mouth and collapse as soon as the sisters left.

"So I'll get to work on these," she said. "As I can, in between my weddings. We'll have another fitting before Christmas, so I can make sure they get done in time for the April wedding."

"Thank you," one of the sisters said, wrapping Ash in a tight hug. They walked out, leaving Zara alone with Ash, who puffed out her cheeks and exhaled.

"They're a handful," Zara agreed, though Ash hadn't said anything.

"I've handled worse, trust me." In fact, Zara's sisters were nothing compared to some of the bridezillas Ash had worked with over the years.

"My mother's already started in on me about my lack of a boyfriend," Zara said. "And then comes the job lecture, blah blah blah."

Ash set her notebook on the desk and took a seat behind it, her heels digging into the top of her right foot uncomfortably. With just Zara in the office, she kicked them off. "Oh, how's the new show? When can I come?"

"It's great." Zara grinned and took a seat across from her. "Come anytime. I can get some tickets for you if you want."

"Two tickets? I'll bring Burke."

Zara's eyebrows went up for a split second before she made a face. "You think he'll like synchronized swimming?"

"It's more than that." Zara was always selling herself short. She was an acrobat, a dancer, and a synchronized swimmer and had managed to find work in half a dozen of Getaway Bay's most popular shows. "We can come anytime. Just tell me when."

"On Tuesdays, you get half-price drink tickets at The Straw with the show."

"Great. Next Tuesday." It was only a few days away, and it would give her and Burke something more to do than lie around and make out—though she liked that just fine too. In fact, her face heated as if Zara could see what she was thinking about.

"Thanks, Ash. You're the best." Zara stood. "I better go catch up to my sisters."

Ash waved and Zara left. Ash sat in her now-quiet office, absorbing the silence and reviving herself with it.

Her bells rang again, and a measure of exhaustion pulled through her. Before she could get up, Burke framed himself in the doorway. "Hey, beautiful." He grinned at her and folded his arms. He wore jean shorts and a T-shirt with a rainbow-colored surfboard on it. "You look like you could use something to eat."

"Desperately." She stood, leaving her heels under her desk. "But can we get it and go home? I'm tired."

"Sure." He glanced around. "Smells like cookies in here." He took a step toward the nearly empty platter, and Ash had just enough energy to lunge in front of him, planting both palms flat against his chest.

"Don't even think about it. Those are mine."

He blinked at her and then burst out laughing. "I'll buy you more cookies," he said once he'd sobered.

"I want the peanut butter cheesecake from Daria's," Ash said, deciding on the spot. She wasn't a huge sweet lover, but on busy days like today, she sure did enjoy something with chocolate and peanut butter. Or chocolate and caramel.

"Daria's is on the other side of the island," Burke said, putting his hands on her hips and bringing her closer.

"Better get going then," she said. "I don't want to be out too late. I have a meeting with a bride in the morning."

Chapter Fifteen

Burke glanced up as a man larger than his father entered his office. "Leo." Burke jumped to his feet like Leo was the King of England. "What are you doing here? Is Gen okay?"

"She's fine." Leo extended his hand for Burke to shake, and then he sat in the chairs lined up against the wall.

Burke had no idea what to do. He'd been reading an article about germination and cross-pollination, and he'd been moments away from nodding off. Now, his heartbeat pulsed against the back of his throat.

"You're serious about Ash?" Leo asked, his dark eyes gazing evenly at Burke.

"I am, Leo. I really like her."

"She hasn't been the luckiest with men."

Burke wanted to say he hadn't exactly had a cakewalk in his romantic past either. Leo really could miss so much sometimes. Instead, he just nodded, a strange expression stuck to his face. He tried to straighten his lips and finally succeeded.

But Leo scowled. "I'm worried about her."

"Why?"

"Remember how you said you were trying to get as many numbers as you could?"

Burke simply blinked at Leo. "I have no idea what you're talking about."

"In high school, you wanted to get all the girls' numbers, so you could text around and find a date whenever you wanted one."

"Okay," Burke said, unsure of what this had to do with now, two decades later, and Leo's sister.

"I didn't want my sister to be one of them."

"I know that, Leo. You made it very clear." He placed his hands flat on his desk the way he'd seen his father do several times in the past. "But we're adults now, and she can make her own decisions."

"As long as you're serious."

"I am."

"It's just that you haven't been very serious about much lately. In a while, actually."

Burke had two advanced degrees. He certainly knew how to work hard, how to achieve something. So maybe he'd been drifting since Bridgette. Did that mean he wasn't responsible?

No, he showed up for work every day—earlier than his father.

Did that mean he couldn't fall in love again?

Every day with Ash proved that wrong.

Leo stood as abruptly as he'd come and said, "If you're sure." He paused, clearly waiting for Burke to say something, but he had no idea what. So Leo just left, and Burke went back to his article on germination.

But his mind lingered far from flowers and pollen and bees. It revolved around what Leo had said, and why he still thought Burke wasn't good enough for Ash.

Because he'd been a bit of a player in high school? Liked to have fun? Go out with different girls? He hadn't gotten serious with any of them. Heck, he was still friends with some of them.

He finally gave up on his reading and left the office in favor of the open sky and long rows of flowers. He walked down the middle lane, the scent of heady perfume hanging in the air.

If you're sure.

Burke wasn't sure of much, honestly. He'd been learning more and more about himself as he spent more and more time with Ash, as they got a little more serious with each passing week.

He now knew he wasn't content with his life. Dolly was great, but she wasn't the only companion he wanted for the rest of his life. He knew he wanted Petals & Leis, and that he wanted to keep the farm in his family for generations to come, just like his dad had expressed.

Sweat trickled down the side of his face, and he turned back to the building so he could stew about his girlfriend, her brother, and what he should do next in the air conditioning.

———

"Burke, your mother's on the phone." His father stood in his office doorway only an hour after Burke had returned from his quick walk through the blooms. Burke glanced at his phone, but the screen was still black.

"In my office." His dad gestured for Burke to come with him.

Seeing no other choice and not wanting to cause a problem, he went. "Hey, Mom," he said as he closed the door. Surely his dad would have the call on speaker.

"Hey," she said. A very long pause came over the group, and she finally said, "George." No question mark at the end, like they'd maybe rehearsed whatever was coming next.

"Your mother would like to set a date for the wedding," his dad said.

Burke blew out his breath. "We don't have a date for the wedding."

"Burke, honey," his mother said. "Our calendar fills up quickly. And when your father retires, we'll do some traveling."

He looked at his father, but he simply settled behind his desk and pulled something toward him as if he had no interest in this conversation. Burke didn't buy it for a moment. His dad had been the one to push him this summer, asking about an engagement ring several times before dropping it without an explanation.

"And Krista called last night and mentioned that she and Tad are getting serious, and they've talked about getting married," his mother continued. "I told her she'd need to consider your feelings. Maybe you won't want to have a wedding too close to yours."

"I don't care when she gets married," Burke said. He hadn't even known she and Tad were serious. The man wasn't serious about much.

Maybe that's a front, Burke thought. Like the one he'd been putting on for years.

"Burke," his mom said again, but his dad interrupted her with, "I think this engagement is a fake."

Burke's eyes flew to his father. His heart raced around inside his chest like he'd injected caffeine straight into the ventricles. He opened his mouth, but nothing came out.

"Burke wouldn't lie to us like that," his mother said over the phone line. His guilt tripled, and Burke didn't know what to say or do.

"Well?" his father challenged.

He cleared his throat, wishing he didn't have to. It made him sound so, so weak—and guilty. "I told you we were going slow," he said.

"Heather, I told you they didn't even really start dating until recently." His dad leaned forward over the speaker on the phone. "There's no way they're engaged."

Anger burned behind Burke's eyes. "How do you know when we started dating?"

His dad looked at him and lifted his chin. "I know a lot of people around town," he said. "You weren't even seen in public together until a couple of weeks before the barbecue."

"They run together every morning," his mom said, and Burke appreciated that she still thought the best of him. He was going to break her heart when he confessed that yes, he'd made up his relationship with Ash because he wanted the flower farm.

"Burke?" his dad pressed.

Burke felt so, so trapped. He hated these walls, the fact that the door was closed behind him. He needed fresh air, and only the sky for a limit.

"Fine. We started dating just before the barbecue. We aren't engaged." His chest heaved. "I'm sorry, Mom." He glared at his father. "I just didn't want to disappoint you. Either of you. And Dad wants to retire, and *I* want Petals and Leis."

His desperation surged, choking back the rest of his words. It felt like lightning had struck in his dad's office. At least he didn't look smug. Just…disappointed. And Burke could only imagine how terrible his mother felt right now.

"I don't see why I have to be married to have the farm," he said. "It feels like a stupid rule."

"We want—"

"The farm to stay in the family. I get it." Burke turned away from his dad, from the conversation. He pulled open the door. "But maybe I'm just not the marrying type. Maybe I'll never find someone I can love like that."

Someone pulled in a sharp breath, and Burke focused his attention out the door to find Ash standing there.

"Ash."

She held a pink pastry box in her hand and a horrified expression on her face. "I knew it," she whispered, shaking her head. Her curls bounced, and it took long seconds for Burke to piece together what she'd said.

"Knew what?"

"That you were pretending." Her eyes filled with tears. "I asked you over and over. Why couldn't you just admit you didn't really like me?"

"What?" Burke took a step toward her at the same time his dad said something. His attention divided, he couldn't form a sentence or make sense of things.

"See?" Ash said. "You did string me along just to keep your farm."

His father joined him just outside his office, and Burke stood there, numb. *That's not true*, he thought but the words wouldn't leave his throat.

"I told myself I'd do whatever I had to do to help you keep Petals and Leis," she said. "But I can't. I deserve to be happy too." She thrust the box toward him, and when he didn't make a move to take it, his father stepped forward and accepted it.

"Happy three-month anniversary." Ash turned on her heel and stormed out.

Only then did Burke feel like he could move and

speak. "Ash, wait," he called after her, finally getting his legs to carry him out of the spot where he'd frozen. He burst outside and ran after her, but she could really move fast when she wanted to.

"Wait," he said, catching her as he arrived at her car.

"It's over, Burke. I don't want to be with you if it's a big lie." She pulled open her car door and got in.

"It's not a lie," he said.

"You just said you won't find someone you'd love enough to marry." She straightened and looked him right in the eye. Not a flinch, or a single ounce of worry sat in her eyes. Burke almost shrank back, and he didn't dare speak.

"Burke, I think you'd know by now if we could be together like that. We've been friends for *so long*." Her voice almost broke, but she contained it. "There's nothing you don't know about me. So what is it? What's holding you back?"

He had no idea.

"I already told you once: I don't want to pretend. And that's all you've been doing." She drew in a deep breath, and he marveled at how she could say exactly what she was thinking. "Good-bye, Burke. Enjoy the doughnuts. Wes said they're your favorite."

She started her car and pulled out of the space, all while Burke's heart wailed and wailed at him to get her *stop! Come back!*

But he said nothing. He'd asked her to wait so he

could explain, but he found he couldn't. What was there to explain?

"Burke."

He spun back to his father, his fury boiling up and up and up. "I'm going home, Dad." He walked away before he said or did something he'd regret for the rest of his life.

As he got in his own car and started it, his phone chimed. He was surprised he even had the device on him, but he did. He pulled it out of his back pocket, almost pulling his shoulder in the process.

It was his mother: *Maybe you're ready for the wedding, but not the marriage.*

He had no idea what that meant. He didn't feel ready for anything, and he certainly didn't want to talk about it.

He did owe his mother an apology, so he sent two simple words and then left the farm, hoping it wasn't for the last time.

Chapter Sixteen

Ash curled into herself, having made it home and into her pajamas. It didn't matter that it was barely lunchtime and she hadn't eaten yet. She'd lost her appetite about the time Burke had lost his voice.

How could he have just stood there and said nothing?

Her breath shuddered as she exhaled, but she held back the tears. She opened her last text from Milo, sent months and months ago.

I'm just not as serious about us as you are.

Anger surged through her, and Ash jammed her finger against the phone until the options came up. She deleted the text stream from Milo, something she should've done a long time ago. Maybe she'd hoped he'd sent the text on a whim.

She'd tried texting him several times after that, but he'd never responded. Never called her again. She'd never heard from him after that, and last she heard, he'd moved to a smaller island to pursue his dreams of writing a novel.

No matter where Milo was, the fact remained that Ash had allowed herself to date another man who wasn't anywhere as serious about them as she was.

"Why?" she asked herself, placing the phone face-down on the bed beside her. "And why Burke?"

Without him, she had no one.

Even as she thought it, she knew it wasn't true. She had friends around the island. Hope and Charlotte. Zara. Even Kayla and Krista would wrap their arms around her and talk bad about their older brother if Ash wanted them to.

She had her family. Leo and Gen and her niece and nephew. Her mother.

So she'd run alone in the morning, along a different beach. Big deal.

But as she rolled onto her back, she knew it was a very big deal. Her phone rang, and she knew who it would be before she even looked at it.

Sure enough, Burke's name and grinning face sat on the screen. She wanted to ignore him, but she wasn't fourteen, so she picked up the phone and answered the call.

"Ash," he said. Nothing else.

She certainly wasn't going to carry this conversation. She'd already said everything on her mind anyway. "You called me, Burke," she said, prompting him in a slightly acidic tone. Maybe very acidic. She wasn't sure she cared at the moment.

"I was not pretending," he said, but his voice lacked its usual oomph.

"You know what, Burke? It doesn't matter." Ash sat up, apparently one more thing to say to him. "You're not ready for a relationship with me. I know it. You know it. Let's just take a break until you figure things out."

"I don't want to take a break."

"Tell me you're over Bridgette."

Burke's hesitation said it all. Ash exhaled, about to do one of the hardest things she'd ever done. "Burke," she said as gently as she could. "Figure things out." She thought maybe she should say she'd still be there once he did, but she didn't know if she would or not.

Maybe her crush would wither by then. Heaven knew Burke didn't do a whole lot very quickly.

In the end, she said, "Call me later," and hung up. How much later he'd call, Ash had no idea. It didn't matter. She'd survived for a couple of years while he was off-island finishing school. And she'd survived seeing him every day when she wanted more than a running partner.

She had plenty to do at work, and she could find other people to spend her free time with. Inspired by the amount of sewing she needed to do, she pulled herself from bed, redressed, and went back to work.

After all, Burke did not get to alter her daily life simply because he'd proclaimed that he'd never want to get married.

As she drove back over to her sewing studio, a tiny voice in her head whispered, *He asked Bridgette to marry him over and over and over.*

So the same conclusion he'd reached about her now applied to Ash.

He wanted to get married. He just didn't want to marry *her*.

———

ASH KEPT HERSELF SO BUSY, SHE COULDN'T DRAG HERSELF out of bed at five a.m. to run. She told herself she wasn't avoiding Burke. She was simply taking care of herself, and she needed more than six hours of sleep, what with the fall wedding on the island coming up. And the bride was wearing her dress and had already posted about it several times on social media.

She called in lunch orders so she wouldn't have to leave her shop. She spent longer and longer hours at her mom's house, even after she'd fallen asleep. And Ash seriously considered getting a dog. Then a cat, as she could leave it home alone for long hours and not have to worry about where it would go to the bathroom.

But she couldn't bring herself to go down to the animal shelter. Was she really going to become the crazy cat lady? She wasn't that hopeless. Was she?

She decided that, no, she wasn't. So no cat. No dog. Nothing to look after but herself, and though she spoke to other people and attended more meetings than she cared to, the loneliness was crushing after only a week.

So she called Charlotte on a day they didn't have a meeting with a bride and said, "Do you have time for lunch?"

"Yes, if we eat it here." She lowered her voice as she said, "Hope's upset about a lost client. Not one of mine, but yeah."

Hope Sorenson owned Your Tidal Forever, and she was usually fair and friendly. But she could get in a bad mood if things went wrong. Ash got it. When she had to unpick an hour's worth of work and start over, she wasn't great company either.

"How do you feel about sushi?" she asked Charlotte.

"Uh, Dawson and I had sushi last night."

"What do you want?" Ash would go anywhere and get anything. She simply couldn't sit in her studio and dine to the sound of her own chewing.

"Pizza?" Charlotte asked. "I know that's not like traditional fare, but I'm tired of all the seafood. I just want a piece of pizza."

Ash smiled. "Hawaiian?"

Charlotte laughed and said, "Whatever. Just bring a lot. It's been a week already and it's only Tuesday."

Ash couldn't agree more, and she agreed to be at Your Tidal Forever in a couple of hours. She pulled out a new bolt of fabric she hadn't cut from yet and rolled it out on the table.

She'd just measured a new bride yesterday, and as

chiffon was a tricky and finicky fabric to work with, she might as well get started today. Other dresses needed to be finished first, but with Ash's new ten-hour days in the shop, she had plenty of time to make her deadlines.

Marking and cutting the fabric, Ash managed to pass the time. Get things done. Mark things off her list. She ordered two pizzas online and left the shop. The September sunshine wasn't quite as brutal as July, but it still leant plenty of heat to the island. She walked down the sidewalk toward the sound of the waves against the shore. After crossing the street, she could get all the way to the water.

A dog barked, making her heart skip a beat. Then two. Was that Dolly? Was Burke here? Getting tacos from Manni's?

Her gaze swept the crowd, but it was impossible to see individuals. And she hated this panic inside her, that she couldn't even walk across the street without worrying over whether she'd see Burke Lawson or not.

She'd lived on this island as long as him, and she shouldn't have to feel restricted in where she went or what she did.

She perched on the edge of the beachwalk and watched the waves in the distance, wishing she were brave enough to leave the island. Maybe I will, she told herself, but her phone chimed out that it was time to go get the pizzas.

So she stood and walked down the street to get those first. She could plan a getaway any time. Right now, she just wanted to eat a meal with someone who didn't ask her why Burke wasn't with her.

Charlotte had piles of paper strewn across her desk when Ash arrived. She looked up, a pair of reading glasses on her nose and said, "Thank the stars," with a heavy sigh. She pressed a button on her desk phone and said, "Riley, she's here."

"I walked right by her desk," Ash said, searching for a place to put down the pizza boxes. "She wasn't there."

"She's hiding out in the back," Charlotte said.

Riley entered a moment later. "I saw her on the security tape." She closed Charlotte's office door behind her. "Hey, Ash."

"Hiding out in the back?" Ash asked.

"Put the pizza here." Charlotte cleared a space on her desk while Riley blew out her breath and rolled her eyes.

"Then I can see when Hope is coming," Riley said. "And still do my job."

"So Hope's not here?" Ash said, setting the pizza on Charlotte's desk.

"No, thank goodness." Riley collapsed into one of Charlotte's chairs. "Did you get the barbecue chicken?"

"No," Ash said, feeling a pinch of guilt for a reason she couldn't name. Maybe because the barbecue chicken was one of Burke's favorites, and she simply didn't want to have anything that reminded her of him.

"I got all-meat and a supreme."

"Both great." Charlotte said, opening both boxes. "I'm starving."

They fell into silence for a few minutes while they ate, and then Charlotte said, "So tell us about what's going on with Burke."

Ash flinched but managed to finish her bite of pizza. "Burke? Nothing's going on with Burke." And that was the sad truth.

Charlotte eyed her but didn't say anything else. Riley finished her pizza and wiped her mouth. "Girl, you were head-over-heels for him. *Something* happened."

"Well, that's true," Ash said. Way too much to tell right now. They only needed the cliff notes anyway. "We broke up a couple of weeks ago. He doesn't want to be serious." Ash wished her chest didn't feel like it was caving in on itself. She wished she could talk about Burke like she used to, like he was a hopeless man who had a good heart.

She seized onto the fact that Burke's heart was good. Sure, maybe it was broken right now, but maybe, just maybe he'd figure out a way to fix it.

"He told you that?" Riley said.

"Said it to his dad," Ash said, "I happened to overhear." She didn't want to go into all the details of how their relationship had started as a mutual agreement, but the fact was, it had. And it still stung every time she thought about it.

"You sound a little bitter," Charlotte said.

"Yeah, well, I really liked him," Ash said, getting a

little choked up on the last word. She shook her head, wishing she'd bought a lot of Diet Coke to go with her pizza. "And it turns out that he just wanted his flower farm."

"What?" Charlotte and Riley asked at the same time, Charlotte adding, "What does that mean?"

"It's nothing," Ash said, shaking her head again. She didn't want to badmouth Burke. "It's nothing. We're nothing. It's over."

And those words sounded final. They sounded true. They sounded like the drawer closing on her plans to ever sew her own wedding dress.

Chapter Seventeen

W hen Burke didn't show up on the bench outside the Petals & Leis administrative offices for a third day in a row, he knew his father would come find him. He ran at a punishing speed, Ash's words on a loop in his head.

Figure things out. Figure things out.

He had no idea how to do that. And she hadn't shown up for their morning run for the third day in a row.

So he ran, and he ran far and long and hard.

When he made it back to his condo, one step through the door told him his father either was there or had been there.

"There you are," he said, confirming that he was still on the premises. He came around the island in the kitchen fully, a cup of coffee in his hand that he'd obviously made while he waited for Burke to show up.

It was fine. Burke hadn't cooked in his kitchen in a very long time. Someone might as well get some use out of the coffee maker.

"Here I am." He took off his T-shirt and used it like a towel on his sweaty head and face. "How long have you been here?"

"Maybe an hour." His father wore sympathy in his eyes, but none of it came through in his voice. He watched Burke, not missing anything, and while Burke had never enjoyed it, today he found it downright obnoxious.

"I'm going to shower." His muscles hurt, and his brain was cranky, and he did not want to talk to his dad.

His dad was the reason he was in this mess with Ash.

No, he thought. *That was all you.*

But it was easier to blame his dad than to figure out where Burke had gone wrong. There were too many choices if he was really going to attempt to analyze what he'd done wrong over the course of the last few months.

"This will just take a moment," his dad said.

Burke paused in his flight toward the hallway that would save his sanity. "What, Dad? What now?"

His dad blinked at him, his eyes hardening. Burke never talked to his father with much disrespect, and he rarely glared as he was now.

"I was just going to say I'm sorry."

"You're—what?"

"Your mother says I put too much pressure on you.

That I made it sound like if you weren't engaged you couldn't have Petals and Leis."

Burke settled his weight and breathed deep, trying to get some reason infused into his brain. "That's exactly what you said."

"Well, I didn't mean it like that. What I wanted to tell you was that we wanted you to have someone to pass the farm to. Someone you meet and fall in love with and want to marry. It doesn't have to be this year or even next. You're young still." He cleared his throat, the very first sign of nerves from his father that Burke had seen in years.

"So." He looked away and sighed. "The farm is still going to be yours come January first. And you can find someone you want to marry, no strings attached. No time frame."

Burke had no idea what to say. This was a completely different father than the one who'd walked with him under the plumeria, expressing his desires for the farm to stay in the family for six more generations.

Had Burke misunderstood him? Or had his father really miscommunicated his ideas so badly?

"All right?" His dad clapped his hand on Burke's shoulder. "You take the time you need to find someone. Maybe it's Ash. Maybe it's not."

Burke's heart crunched inside his chest, but his dad grabbed him and gave him a hug. "I love you, son." His voice tumbled through Burke's chest, ragged and gruff as his father didn't express himself or how he was feeling all that often.

No wonder Burke had a hard time doing the same thing.

———

A WEEK LATER, BURKE STILL HAD NO IDEA WHAT TO DO about Ash. Then two weeks passed, and all he seemed to be able to do was run, go into work, and stay until lunch. Then he'd wander around the beach for a while until he thought of something he wanted to eat.

He didn't admit to himself until the second week that he was wandering the area closest to Ash's sewing studio, hoping to see her. Casually run into her. Maybe drag her behind Manni's again and kiss her until she believed that he hadn't pretended with her.

By the beginning of the third week, he was done moping around. Ash had said to call her later, when he had things figured out, and it was time to get that done.

His first stop: Leo.

Burke felt like a complete idiot driving up the winding roads to Leo's new, sprawling mansion. Only billionaires lived up here; men like Marshall Robison, the owner of the largest pineapple plantations on the island.

But Leo opened the door wearing a pair of joggers and a T-shirt, clearly having just completed a workout. "Hey, man." He shook Burke's hand and added, "We can meet in my office." He led the way down the hall and into a room with the largest desk Burke had ever seen. And with Leo behind it in such informal clothing almost made Burke scoff.

Leo simply looked at him, and Burke supposed he had called his best friend and asked if they could meet.

"So I'm sure you heard about me and Ash." The whole company knew, which meant the entire island did too.

"Gen mentioned something about a double chocolate doughnut and why she got to bring it home."

"I'm surprised you didn't call," Burke said. "Come beat me up."

"It's…." Leo exhaled heavily. "I thought about it, but then I remembered my sister's face when she told me it was none of my business. And it's not. She made her choice, and she'll have to deal with it."

"Deal with what?"

"You breaking her heart."

Instant fury shot through Burke. "Try the other way around."

Leo opened his mouth to say something, then closed it again. "I'm sorry, what? Are you saying you fell for her?"

Burke scoffed. "Of course not. I mean, I liked her." He felt like he was on a slippery slope, about to lose his footing and then lose everything else. "She said I was pretending. But I wasn't. Leo, I swear I wasn't."

He simply wasn't sure he could fall in love again.

All at once, he knew what he needed to figure out. And wasn't that half the battle?

He stood, said, "Thanks, Leo," and started to leave.

"Thanks for what?" Leo called after him, but Burke didn't turn back or try to explain. He had to figure out how to get over Bridgette so he could find out if he could love Ash.

And if not, at least he'd know. At least maybe he could salvage their friendship. He was tired of running alone. Tired of waking up alone. Tired of being alone.

And not just alone. But without Ash.

He now had two lives—with Ash and this new one where he didn't have her. No one to talk to. No one to just be with while the sun sank into the ocean and she talked about her mom.

Burke didn't want someone else to share those things with. He wanted his friendship with Ash.

And maybe more, if he could open his heart to the possibility of…getting hurt again.

He started his car and began the winding drive back down to the water's edge. "That's what you have to decide," he told himself. "Whether or not you're willing to get hurt again. Ask her to marry you and be told no one more time."

His heart pulsed once, twice. A clear warning that it did not want to be hurt again. That it still had old scars he hadn't dealt with.

"How do I deal with them?" he asked himself, a

measure of desperation in his voice that mirrored how he felt inside.

In any other situation, he'd go to see Ash. Ask her what she thought, and then he'd do what she said.

He pulled to a stop at a red light, wondering if he really could turn left and wind through the beach community until he pulled up to her cottage. She wouldn't be there anyway. He'd been running by her house in the morning, and no matter how early he got there, her car was gone already.

He knew where she was, and his fingers flexed on the steering wheel. Could he just show up in her sewing studio and ask her for her advice? Would she even talk to him?

She *had* picked up the phone when he'd called, weeks ago. She *had* said "call me later."

And she didn't like drop-ins. So he should definitely call first. But if he called first, and she said he couldn't come....

Burke yanked the wheel to the right, earning him a honk from the car behind him. "I can't do it," he said to himself, wondering when he'd decided to be one of those people that talked to themselves in their car. "I can't go through another day without Ash."

Apparently *today* he needed her back.

He pulled into the parking lot that served the strip mall where her shop sat. He had no plan, and if there was anything he'd learned from all of his botched proposals to Bridgette, it was that a man should have a plan.

He put the car in reverse, ready to back out. Then pushed it back into park. He couldn't go back to his house tonight. Lie on his own couch. He just couldn't do it.

"Time to face her," he muttered to himself, and he got out of the car. The bells on her front door would alert her to someone's presence, and he could judge her mood and level of exhaustion by how fast she appeared in the doorway where she worked.

He put his hand on the handle and drew in a deep breath. "Now or never," he told himself, wondering what that really meant. Because if he didn't go inside now, he certainly could tomorrow.

Maybe.

If he had the nerve.

So he better just get it over with now.

He opened the door, the bells ringing.

And then he counted.

Chapter Eighteen

Ash had taken to playing loud music while she sewed. The activity had soothed her more than any other since the age of twelve, but she'd done it so often, large parts of her brain were open for thinking even while she stitched together difficult pieces and types of fabric.

The music helped drown out any thoughts that might sneak in, specifically about Burke. She could keep the fabric under the needle with her eighties pop music in the background, and she got a lot more accomplished when she could just focus on the work.

"Too busy to talk for a minute?" a man yelled, making her jerk, her foot coming off the pedal but her needle still going awry. Great. Now that seam would need to be redone.

She lifted her eyes to the doorway. Burke stood there.

Or a heavenly vision of him, because it certainly couldn't actually *be* him.

Could it?

Ash stumbled to her feet, one foot still in her wedged sandal and one shoeless as she sewed. She braced herself against the table, her heart thundering in her chest like a racehorse's hooves.

"Burke?" She searched for the remote to the stereo, finding it on the edge of the table and lunging for it. She hit it with her hand, sending it flying across the hard floor. Somehow, even over the music, she heard the crack of plastic against the laminate, and the cover for the battery bounced free.

Burke said something she didn't catch among the lyrics, and he moved toward the remote control at the same time she hobbled after it too. When it became clear he was going to reach it first, she paused where she was. Getting too close to him would be dangerous.

He bent and picked it up, fitting the cover back over the batteries. Pointing the remote toward the wall, he pushed a button. Nothing happened. The Bangles continued to sing about their manic Monday.

He tried another spot, and another press of the button. The music continued to blast, and Ash stutter-stepped over to him and took the remote from him, being very careful not to breathe or touch him.

"I just wanted to talk," he said, but she moved away before she could get even a note of his cologne. Ash tried pressing the power button to silence the whole radio, but again, nothing happened.

She took off the battery cover and made sure the power supply was properly seated. It was. And still pressing a button did nothing.

"Where is it?" Burke yelled over the chorus.

"Where's what?" Ash looked directly at him, which was a huge mistake. Because even though the music continued to blare, everything slowed and stopped in that heartbeat. The moment lengthened, and she lost herself in those blue, oceanic eyes, giving herself the moment she'd missed so much these past few weeks.

"The stereo?" He gestured like it should be mounted to the wall.

"Oh." Ash turned in a full circle, feeling like she was doing a weird pony dance with the different heights due to her shoeless foot. "It's in that cabinet." Which was very high up, near the ceiling. She couldn't reach it, and though Burke had a few inches on her, he wouldn't be able to without a chair or ladder either.

The song ended, and the fraction of second before the announcer spoke brought a brief respite. Burke said, "I just wanted—" before the man started speaking again, detailing the weather for later that day and into the weekend.

"—to talk," Burke said loudly. Another song started to play, and it wasn't the calm, ballady type they could talk over, but more of a rock jam Ash used to dance around to when she was younger.

"I can't keep doing this," he said, yelling over the drums and guitars. "I need your advice. I can't figure things out without you, because *you're* who'd I go to when I need to talk things through."

Ash folded her arms, her senses completely over-loaded. "Not true. You never talked to me about Bridgette."

Frustration rolled across his expression. "I was embarrassed about Bridgette. You knew anyway."

"Some stuff," Ash said, unsure about why she was arguing with him about this, of all things. But he had not told her he'd proposed to her, not even once. And he'd done it over and over again.

Burke looked away, his gaze eventually migrating back to hers. "I don't know what to do. *You* always help me figure out what to do."

Even with the pounding song, she heard the desperation in his words. It tugged against her heart, pulling harder and harder with every passing moment. But her heart resisted, though she did want to work things out with him.

But not this version of him.

She shook her head and backed up a step. "I'm not helping you figure this out. This is a Burke issue you need to identify and solve."

"I know the issue."

"Yeah? What is it?"

"What?"

"What is it?" she yelled over the guitar riff.

Burke didn't say anything, just as Ash suspected he would. Burke didn't say a whole lot about what he was feeling; he never had. Emotions stormed across his face though, and Ash got the answers she needed from that.

"If you're still in love with her—"

"I'm not," Burke said, the words loud and powerful. "I'm not, Ash." The song ended, but he continued in his near-yell, "I'm in love with you."

She stared at him, sure her brain had been muddled because of the loud eighties rock song. Sure the ringing in her ears had made his words vibrate and reform into something they weren't.

The announcer came back on, and Ash really needed everything to be silent so she could think. "I have to go," she said, kicking off her other wedge and heading toward the exit.

"Ash," Burke said behind her, but she fled as fast as her bare feet and narrow pencil skirt would let her. The fall sunshine hit her, and she stumbled when her feet hit the hot cement. But she kept going.

She was *not* going to give Burke advice on how to make up with her.

And he doesn't love you.

Her mind wouldn't let go of the words though, spoken in his voice.

I'm not, Ash.

I'm in love with you.

―――――

Ash didn't return to her sewing studio until that evening, and she wore a pair of leggings, an oversized T-shirt with a giant flower on the front, and sneakers. The door was locked, which would've been thoughtful and considerate of Burke had Ash not left her keys inside. She cupped her hands and peered through the glass. All the lights had been turned off, and she couldn't hear any music, so he must've figured out how to silence that blasted stereo at some point.

She turned to leave, vowing to wait until morning to call a locksmith. Then she wouldn't have to pay the after-hours fee. But her foot slipped on something, and she found an envelope beneath her right foot.

Her heart jumped as if it had transformed into a rabbit, and she bent to pick up the envelope. It had her name on it in Burke's messy script, and she simultaneously wanted to rip it open and read it and toss it in the nearest fire.

But as there were no fires nearby, Ash pinched the envelope in her fingers. She glanced up and down the street like someone would be there to arrest her for looking in a window—a window she owned—and picking up a piece of paper.

No one even seemed to notice her standing there. She made it back to her car and shoved the envelope in her purse before heading up into the hills to her mother's house.

Her bag felt like a lead weight as she shouldered it and took it inside. Her mom stood at the stove already, onions and red peppers sautéing while she chopped a green pepper to add to the pan.

"Hey, Mom." Ash set her purse with the envelope in it on the counter and leaned over to give her mom a kiss.

"There you are." She turned and wiped her hands on her apron. "I was beginning to worry."

"You were?" Ash glanced at the clock on the stove. "I'm not even late." She still smoothed her hands down her hips as if she'd done something wrong by stopping by her shop before coming straight up here.

Her mom turned back to the stove and scooped the green peppers into the pan. "Burke came by," she said as if she was discussing the size of her pumpkins in the garden.

Ash sucked in a breath. "Burke? Came here?"

"He was looking for you. Seemed a bit panicked, honestly. Wanted me to tell you he'd stopped by, and that you left your phone and keys in your shop. He's got them."

"He's got them? Like, what? He's holding them hostage?"

Her mom turned away from the vegetables again. "What?"

"We broke up, Mom. Weeks ago." Ash paced out of the small kitchen, the outdoors calling to her in a way they never had before. She didn't want to have this conversation right now. Not today. Probably not ever.

"You broke up?" Her mom came after her and touched her shoulder. Ash faced her, wishing she didn't feel like her whole world had collapsed without Burke to keep her steady. "Oh, and I can see it's not a good thing."

"I really liked him, Mom." Ash's voice sounded like she'd just taken in a large lungful of helium. In the next moment, her face crumpled, and Ash started crying.

She hadn't cried once since she'd broken up with Burke, and it felt like weeks and months and years of tears came streaming out of her.

"I really liked him."

Her mom gathered her into an embrace, and Ash clung to her, glad and grateful she was still here in this critical time, but wishing Ash could fix things for Burke, because then she'd be able to fix things between them too.

Chapter Nineteen

Burke stared at the shop keys sitting next to Ash's phone on his front table. Darkness had claimed the island at least an hour ago, and while she'd been staying up at her mother's long past this time, surely she knew by now that he had her belongings.

"Just take them back to her," he muttered to himself. She wouldn't come to him, he knew that.

So he swiped the keys and her phone and left his condo. He wasn't going to hide out behind closed doors and make her come asking for what belonged to her.

"Come on, Dolly," he said, and the golden retriever lifted her head like they'd be going to a party. Burke loaded the sixty-pound dog into his car and drove over to Ash's place. Her windows were dark, but Dolly whined, so he got out and let the dog out.

She sniffed around, finally finding the perfect place to

do her business, and then she jumped up the steps and circled until she found a good spot for lying on the cement.

"We're not staying," Burke said to her as he climbed the few steps and opened the screen door. Her keys and phone would be safe there, and she'd find them when she got home. Having placed her items between the screen door and the front door, he turned to leave.

He tried to breathe in, but it was so, so hard. His chest felt like someone had wrapped an industrial rubber band around his lungs and was twisting so tight, so tight.

He choked but somehow managed to get himself down the steps and back to his car. "Come on," he said to his dog, but she didn't move. He took a couple of steps back around the front of the car and called for the dog again.

She still wouldn't come, and Burke had had enough of this day. "Fine, whatever." Even his dog wanted Ash more than him, and Burke found himself in the same camp.

He got in the car and sent her a text. *Dolly wouldn't come with me, so can you keep her for the night? Just set her on the sand in the morning and she'll find me.*

He didn't want to think about Ash being on the same sand he was while he ran alone. He wondered if she'd been going to the gym—which she hated—and his heart clenched.

"She can make her own choices," he told himself,

starting the car and pulling away from her house. He watched his rearview mirror, half hoping Ash would pull up, see him, and they'd get to talk.

It didn't matter. He'd already said what he'd needed to say. Well, part of it. And she'd stood there and blinked. Then she'd run away.

At least Bridgette had never done that. She'd stayed and said no right to his face.

Bitterness filled him, and Burke was really glad there were no headlights behind him. He didn't want to talk to Ash when he was angry. Or bitter. Or wishing he knew what to say or do.

He was going to figure things out.

That didn't happen the next morning, but at least Ash texted back that Dolly wouldn't leave her side, even when she ran down to the water and back. Even when she'd told the retriever to go find Burke.

So I'll just keep her for a while if that's all right.

Burke didn't particularly like the idea. Dolly had been the only thing keeping him company since the break up. The only living creature who listened to him at night, who laid by him and reminded him that he wasn't utterly alone.

But he had no other choice but to respond with *All right*, and let the retriever stay with her.

He ran on the beach, and he walked through the flower fields as they prepped some for the cooler winters in Hawaii. He participated in another late plumeria harvest, and he went over the documents with his father that would make the farm his, no strings attached.

"So you just need to sign there," the manager at the bank said. He was acting as the notary for the paperwork, and Burke held the pen, ready to sign.

He met his father's eye. "Ready?" his dad asked, a fond smile appearing on his face. "You're totally ready for this, Burke. You've learned everything you need to know about the farm, and you're *ready*."

Burke felt ready, and he signed his name on the paperwork, watched as it got stamped and sealed, and when he and his father left the bank, Burke finally felt like he'd done something right in his life.

He felt more grown up than he ever had, and another piece of himself fell into place. He'd been gathering them slowly as the days and weeks passed, as the children in Getaway Bay went trick-or-treating, as pumpkin pie was made and served, and as Christmas decorations went up and down Main Street.

So maybe Burke drove by the little strip of shops where Ash sewed. But he didn't stop, not again. He knew the holiday season was extremely busy for her, and while he still didn't have his dog back, he was slowly starting to feel more and more like himself.

The real Burke. The one he'd been before the warped version of Burke Lawson had emerged as he'd tried to win Bridgette's heart.

He found a piece when he figured out which restaurants were his favorite. His. Not where Bridgette wanted to eat. He found a piece when he took over the farm and the employees threw him a party and welcomed him as if he had the knowledge and experience to be their boss.

He found a piece as he ran on the beach by himself, because he learned how to *be* by himself.

He thought a lot about Ash and what he might say to her. Nothing came to mind, so he didn't go see her and didn't text her. He even stopped looking for her or Dolly in the morning while he stretched.

He went to a New Year's Eve party with DJ, one of the first parties he'd been to in a very long time. The other man moved seamlessly through the crowds, leaning into the pretty women and giving them a kiss on the cheek.

Burke felt very out of his element, and while he liked DJ and had gotten to know the man better over the past few months, he didn't want to be at this party.

"Burke," a woman said as he trailed in DJ's wake, and he turned toward her.

The woman in front of him was familiar, but he couldn't remember her name. "Hey," he said, the word falling falsely from his mouth. He really hated that. "I'm sorry," he said next. "I don't remember your name."

"Vivien," she said, her face falling the slightest bit. "We went to the hospital gala together a few years ago."

Understanding hit him, and he remembered the black tie event his father had suggested he attend, as the farm had donated some money for the new children's wing. "Oh, of course." He smiled at her, keeping his attention on her though he wanted to glance around for an escape. "Good to see you."

"You too." Vivien stood there, sipping her drink and scanning the crowd beyond him.

And that was when Burke knew that he was going to leave this party and do whatever it took to get the life he wanted. "I'm sorry," he said with another smile. "I have to go."

He walked away from Vivien and right on out of the party. Not wanting to be rude, he did text DJ and then he called for a ride home. As he walked up the steps to his condo building, he felt like he was ready to make this year the best one of his life yet.

He just needed to find a way to get Ash back into that life.

———

A couple of days later, he drove the delivery truck to the airport and restocked the Petals & Leis kiosk there. Once everything was set, he started back toward the farm, taking a detour past Ash's place.

He still had no ideas for what he should say or do, but he did see a flash of golden fur as he passed *Dress of Your Dreams*, and that caused him to brake. "She's taking Dolly to the shop?"

That animal shed more hair than any dog alive, and there was no way that wasn't getting all over the dresses.

He went around the block and pulled into the parking lot. He found a spot a few doors down, but the glare from the sun made it impossible to see if Dolly was indeed inside the shop.

He pulled out his phone and sent a text to Ash. *How's Dolly? Driving you nuts? I can pick her up anytime.*

A few minutes passed before his phone lit up. *She's fine. I'll drop her off at your place. Thanks for letting me keep her so long.*

He wanted to continue the conversation, but he took a moment to analyze *why* he wanted to keep talking to her.

Because what he'd blurted in her shop was still true. He was still in love with her.

Are you running at the gym? he typed out.

No, came her single-word response.

Want to meet me at the beach tomorrow? he typed out but didn't send. Did he dare send it? What would she say? Could he handle it if she said no?

Once again, Burke sat back and took a few moments to think.

He sent his text, sure his heart could handle a rejection from her. Because it was whole again, and he was ready to do whatever it took to get her back.

Ash didn't respond, and Burke backed out of the parking space and continued back up to his farm.

The next morning, he arrived at his and Ash's usual meeting spot earlier than usual and went through his pre-run stretching routine twice before admitting to himself she wasn't going to come. And then there was also the fact that he might never get his dog back.

He'd started out at a slow jog when he heard a dog bark. Stalling, he turned back and scanned the golden sand, searching for Dolly.

She came tearing toward him, sand flying up from her paws, and Burke laughed. "Come on," he called, and she ran right up to him, her tail wagging her whole body. "How are you, huh, girl? I haven't seen you in so long."

He knelt down and scrubbed Dolly, happier to see her than he cared to admit. "Oh, you smell good. Has Ash been giving you a bath? Has she? Huh?"

"I tried, once."

Burke looked up to see Ash standing there, and if the sun had been up, it would've haloed her. As it was, her presence made his entire soul light up and he slowly rose to his feet.

"You didn't answer my text," he said.

"Yeah." She looked at him, and Burke couldn't stand the charge between them.

"I'm so sorry," he said. "I've been figuring things out, and I'm—"

She reached up and touched her forefinger to his lips, effectively silencing him.

"I have a few things to say," she said. "Apparently, I

had a few things to figure out too." Her hand fell from his mouth, and Burke felt like she'd branded him.

When they stood there standing for several long seconds, staring, Burke said, "Go on, then," hoping with everything in him that what she had to say were things like *I'm sorry I kept your dog for so long*, and *I love you too*.

Chapter Twenty

Ash couldn't believe she stood on the beach with Burke Lawson. Sure, she'd run with him hundreds of times. Probably thousands. But none of their mornings had started like this.

"I'm just as much to blame as you are," she said. "I shouldn't have acted like our relationship was real when it was only an agreement."

"Ash," he said, but she held up her hand, and he didn't continue. That was new. The old Burke would've said what he wanted.

This man before here was a completely different man with the same flop of gorgeous blond hair and those eyes.

Oh, yes, those eyes would always be her undoing.

"I knew we needed to go slow, but I was so convinced you weren't being genuine with me."

"I was," he whispered.

"I know that now. I've never eaten so many tacos in my life."

Burke opened his mouth to say something and then shut it again. A frown creased his eyebrows. "I'm sorry. Tacos?"

"DJ's been giving me little tidbits about what you've been up to." A smile stretched her face. "You took over the farm?"

He nodded, a slip of hardness entering his eyes. "Yes, a couple of weeks ago." He looked over her shoulder and back to her. "You've been spying on me through DJ?"

"I think I've gained fifteen pounds eating the pork tacos." She laughed, though her wardrobe was indeed tighter than it used to be. "But the guacamole there is…." She shook her head. "Unbelievable."

Burke chuckled too, breaking all the tension between them.

"I'm sorry," Ash said, her stomach lurching. "I may have expected more from you than you were capable of giving."

"I'm capable now." He took a step toward her, and Ash's skin tingled in anticipation of being touched by him.

"Are you?"

"I've been gathering up all the pieces of my heart," he said. "And listening to it. And Ash, I'm still in love with you."

A grin burst onto Ash's face, as Burke seemed to

know exactly what to say and what Ash needed to hear. "I love you, too."

He smiled, stepped again, and trailed his fingers over hers and up her arm to her elbow. "Can we maybe try again?" he asked, moving closer and bending down so the tip of his nose touched her temple. Her heart beat wildly out of control as her blood heated.

"No agreements," she said.

"No agreements," he said. "Just me and you figuring things out together." His hands slipped around her, and Ash tipped her head back to look into his eyes. Have her moment.

After taking it, she stretched up onto her toes and paused with her mouth only inches from his. "I'm going to kiss you now," she whispered.

"Go on, then." He closed his eyes and waited, looking beyond handsome and peaceful at the same time.

She did, and the moment her lips touched his, everything that had been seething inside her these past few months calmed.

———

ONLY TWENTY MINUTES LATER, SHE SLOWED HER JOG TO A walk, her calves screaming and her breath burning on the way in and out of her lungs. "Wow," she panted. "I'm completely out of shape."

Burke ran back to her and around her. "So you didn't go running at all since we broke up?"

Ash shook her head, still trying to get a proper amount of oxygen. It seemed like with the change of the seasons that maybe the island had suddenly increased in elevation.

"Why not?" Burke asked, finally coming to a rest on both feet.

"Reminded me too much of you," she said honestly, wanting everything between them to be filled with honesty from now on. She added a shrug to the statement so he wouldn't know how terribly she'd missed him. Keeping his dog had probably told him that already.

"I drove by your shop all the time," he said. "It was as close to you as I could get." He drew her close to him now, and she drew in a deep breath of the scent of his laundry detergent and enjoyed the feel of his arms around her.

"You sure took a long time figuring things out." Ash looked up at him, hoping for more of an explanation.

"Yeah." He exhaled, laced his fingers through hers, and said, "Can we walk at least?"

Ash could definitely walk, so she did that. She'd also need to lay off the tacos and figure out a workout regimen so she could get back in good enough shape to run the miles and miles Burke did. That she once had.

"I had to go step by step," Burke said, his voice thoughtful. "See, my heart was in a lot of pieces, and I had to find them all and put them all back together."

Ash took a few more steps before she said, "I had no

idea you were so poetic." She giggled, simply glad not to be running.

"Don't laugh," he said, though he chuckled too. "I figured out that I was afraid of being rejected again. That's why I didn't want another relationship."

Ash held his hand, knowing she had some confessions of her own to voice. "I didn't believe you could really like me," she said. "So I've spent the last few months trying to figure out why I thought that."

"And?" he prompted.

"Milo," she said.

"I told you that guy was an idiot."

Ash half laughed and half sighed. "He wasn't serious about anything, and I am. Well, you know how I am."

"Wonderful?" He pressed a kiss to her forehead. "Hardworking? Beautiful?"

"Serious," she said, though she appreciated the compliments. "I've sort of had to be, what with my mother getting sick when I was so young."

"I like you," he said. "Just how you are."

"Thank you," she murmured, the water getting a little too close to her sneakers. "And you're different."

"I figured out who I am," he said. "And I'm just warning you, you might not like every piece anymore."

"I never liked every piece."

"Ouch." He chuckled, and Ash stepped in front of him.

"I mean it, Burke. You're a great guy, but I knew you weren't being real."

He gazed down at her, dozens of emotions flying through his eyes. "Why didn't you say something?"

"Say something? What would you have liked me to say? 'Burke, you've lost your motivation.'?"

"Well, maybe not that." He grinned and bent down to kiss her again. Before he did, he paused and said, "I'm sorry about Milo. But I *am* serious about you." And he kissed her like he meant it.

———

ELEVEN MONTHS LATER:

The bell on Ash's shop sounded, but she didn't get up from the sewing machine. She couldn't believe her own gown had proven to be so dang difficult to construct. But she wanted beads, and lace, and chiffon. The multi-layers had kept her at the machine past her normal quitting time for weeks now, and her big day was in only a few days.

"Hey." Burke entered the room, the scent of Chinese food coming with him. "I come bearing egg rolls and that spicy chicken you love." He set the food on the table across from her and came around the sewing desk to give her a quick kiss on the back of her neck.

His lips lingered there, and she let up on the pedal as a slow heat filled her from head to toe. The needle stopped, and she reached back and ran her fingers through Burke's hair as he continued to kiss her.

She laughed, spun in her chair, and kissed her fiancé

like she couldn't wait to say *I do* in only a few days. Which, of course, she couldn't.

"Come eat," he said, slipping away from her. "You can work faster after you've had some calories."

She'd tried arguing this point with him in the past, and he'd called her "crabby and cranky" when she didn't eat in favor of staying at the machine. Plus, she didn't want to. With her own wedding this Christmas season, Ash thought she may have bitten off more than she could sew for the first time.

"Em's coming in the morning," she said, sighing as she sat in the chair next to where Burke was unloading the food he'd brought. "Final fitting. I should be able to finish that tomorrow. And Chesney's wedding is on Thursday, and her dress is done. And Willow's isn't for three weeks after ours, but I want her dress as close to done as possible so I'm not stressing while we're on our honeymoon."

"Sounds good." He opened a container and pushed it toward her when she saw it held noodles. "And how's your dress coming?" He glanced toward the heap of white fabric on the sewing desk.

Ash hadn't wanted him to see the dress, but she literally had to work on it at all hours, and she couldn't turn Burke away after they'd spent all day working apart. It wasn't like he could tell how magnificent it would be when it was in shambles, as it currently was.

"It's…coming." She dumped almost the entire container of noodles onto her paper plate and reached for the spicy chicken. "I think I'll be able to finish it, but it's going to be tight." And she didn't just mean that she'd managed to lose the fifteen pounds she'd gained during their break up, but that she may have overestimated how narrow her waist really was.

So she ate half of the noodles and only a few pieces of the chicken before she positioned herself behind the sewing machine again. If she could just get this gauzy, airy, beautiful fabric to line up and stay in place, she could get this dress done lickety-split.

He pulled her away from the work once more when he decided to go home. "Dolly will be wondering where I am." He bent over and pressed a kiss to her forehead, and Ash took a moment to admire him as he walked out.

Then she got back to work.

Chapter Twenty-One

"It's too tight," Burke wanted to wrench the tie off his neck and throw it as far as he could. "Leo, it's too tight."

"It's supposed to be tight." His friend bumped his hand away from where Burke was trying to rip the bow tie off.

"I'm sure that's not right," Burke said. "They come in sizes, don't they?"

The door behind him opened and his dad entered, carrying a box with a red ribbon. "That better be a pair of scissors," Burke said.

His dad grinned at him. "No, but your mother insisted you have this before the ceremony."

Burke couldn't wait for the ceremony to be over, because then Ash would be his wife and they would be alone. It felt like a decade had passed since that morning on the beach instead of only a year.

He'd asked her to marry him on the same beach, months after she'd gotten her running mojo back. He'd worked for six months to train Dolly to dig in a certain spot and when she had and procured the ring, Burke had dropped to both knees and popped the question.

Thankfully, Ash had said yes almost before he'd finished his sentence.

Burke lost himself in the memory for a moment. It had been so fantastic to finally hear that yes from the woman he loved. She'd gotten a little teary, and Burke had to admit that he almost had too.

Now he just hoped she'd show up.

She'll show up, he told himself. *She said yes.*

"Open it," Leo said, interrupting Burke's memories and thoughts. "You don't want to be late going downstairs."

Ash had wanted a beach wedding, complete with silver bells and gold stars for the Christmas holiday. She'd hired her friend Charlotte at Your Tidal Forever, and he could look out the window and see the branch wreaths covered in twinkling tea lights, the white fabric that looked like gauze which flowed over the chairs and altar. The splashes of navy and deep crimson on the chairs and altar, along with the metallic elements.

He pulled the ribbon off the box and found a pair of cufflinks inside. "Dad?"

"They were mine, at my wedding," he said. "And your grandfather's before that. And his father's before that. As long as Petals and Leis has been in our family, so have these cufflinks." His dad lifted the first one out of the box and helped Burke put it on. Once both cufflinks were in place, Burke lifted his wrist to see them in the mirror.

"They have little flowers on them," he said, turning them this way and that to see the orchid.

"My dad had those engraved." His dad started fiddling with Burke's bow tie, miraculously loosening it. "There, that's got to be better. Your whole face was turning red."

Burke glared at Leo, who simply laughed. "I don't wear bow ties," he said by way of explanation.

Someone knocked on the door four times, sharply, and then a woman poked her head into the room. "Good, you're dressed. Five minutes, Mister Lawson." The wedding planner left, and Burke drew in a deep breath.

"All right. Let's do this." He checked his hair one more time, glad this December day wasn't too terribly windy. He went downstairs and outside, the scent of plumeria and orchid hitting him square in the chest the same way the humidity did. Huge urns of the flowers stood at the end of the aisle and edged the entire section of the beach where their wedding would take place.

He smiled at the blooms, appreciating that Ash had given such a major nod to him and his family. Almost everyone had already taken their seats, and his mother stood to look at him from head to toe. "You got the cufflinks?"

He showed them to her and gave both of his sisters a hug. The preacher gestured him forward and started explaining how things would go. Burke had been through it before, at the rehearsal just last night. He knew where to stand. He knew where to look for the photographer. He couldn't wait for the actual wedding to be done.

But he stood in his spot, his cells buzzing with anticipation, excitement, and if he were being honest —anxiety.

She said yes. She said yes. She said yes.

And then she came out of the same door he had, someone holding the train of her dress while she adjusted the bodice. Though she was farther away than he would've liked, he basked in her beauty, in the honor she'd given him by placing an orchid in her hair, in the absolute joy now soaring through him.

Her wedding party swallowed the sight of her, and they stayed as a wall in front of her as they moved her into position at the back of the congregation. Her bridesmaids moved down the aisle, latching onto a groomsman after the first row of chairs.

Finally, everyone was in position, and Ash stood at the end of the aisle with her brother. Leo looked at her, and she looked at him, and they both faced Burke.

Step by step, she walked toward him, a radiant smile on her face. Leo passed her to Burke, and the entire crowd faded in her brilliance. Only she existed on the beach with him, and Burke took a deep drag of her perfume before facing the preacher.

"Friends and family, welcome to the marriage of Burke David Lawson and Ashley Cynthia Fox…."

Burke tried to pay attention, he really did. But all he could focus on was the feel of Ash's hand against his arm, and the way she seemed to be made of sunlight and stars while she read her vows to him.

He read his, and the pastor said, "I now pronounce you man and wife."

And then Burke got to do what he'd been waiting so long to do: he kissed his wife.

———

Read on for sneak peek at THE ISLAND HIDEAWAY, Book 3 in the Getaway Bay series.

Sneak Peek! The Island Hideaway
Chapter One

Z ara Reddy pulled her dark hair out of its ponytail, the amount of water squeezing out with her elastic making a huge puddle on the floor. She was used to being wet, because she worked as a synchronized swimmer on the island on Getaway Bay, in some of their most popular shows.

This summer's show kept her busy with practices during the week, and nightly shows from Thursday to Sunday. She didn't work the matinees, thankfully. She was grateful for the jobs that always seemed to come her way. That way, she didn't have to go to work at her family's Indian restaurant in downtown Getaway Bay.

They were traditional in every sense of the word, and Zara had made more explanations about her life choices over the years than she cared to admit.

Her phone flashed violently with blue and green

lights, and she checked her texts first as the other swimmers came into the locker room.

"Are you coming with us to dinner?" Suzie asked, taking Zara's attention from her device.

"Oh, uh, I don't think so," she said, lifting her phone. "I think I just got that housesitting job."

Suzie wrung out her hair and started changing. "That's great, Zee. Up on the bluffs?"

"Yeah. First time." She was an experienced house sitter, and she'd completed a dozen or so jobs now. It was easy work, and she got to stay in some of the nicest houses on the island.

And this one?

This one was the crown jewel of the mansions up on the bluff. She'd been texting back and forth with a woman named Petra for several days now, and Zara had never answered so many questions. It was house sitting, not rocket science.

But Petra wanted a background check, and Zara's references, and if there would be any pets in the house. Zara did have a long-haired white cat, but she'd kept that to herself. Petra didn't seem like the kind that would tolerate felines.

The pay was sky high, and Zara smiled as she tapped out her acceptance of the job. She had a small apartment in a long row of them, and staying up on the bluffs would add to her gasoline bill, but it would be so much better than listening to the thirty-somethings next door try to become Hawaii's next big boy band—at all hours of the night.

The address to the house appeared on her screen, along with the code to the gate and the garage. *Anytime tonight or tomorrow*, Petra said. *Send me your PayMe, and I'll get you the money.*

Zara showered and dressed, throwing her heavy bag full of suits, props, caps, nose clips, goggles, and more over her shoulder and heading out to her car. Hopefully, it would start. It was much too hot to sit in the car without air conditioning, listening to the engine click while she prayed it would turn over.

"With this new job," she muttered to herself as she crossed the parking lot. "You can maybe afford to buy a new car." One that actually started the first time.

Sighing, she got behind the wheel and stuck in the key. Miraculously, the car started with the first turn, and she fiddled with the dials on the air conditioner to make it blow harder. Her phone rang, and she answered the call from one of her best friends, Ash Fox.

"Hey, Ash." Zara put the car in reverse, trying not to let any of the jealousy she'd been experiencing when it came to Ash infuse her voice. See, Ash had been Zara's go-to friend when everyone else had a boyfriend. Ash never did. Ash sat behind her sewing machine almost all the time. Zara could always count on Ash—until Burke.

And now Zara had a huge, empty house on the bluffs to go home to.

"So remember how you said you might be able to help out at Your Tidal Forever?" Ash asked.

"Yeah," Zara said slowly.

"Well, Hope is *swamped,* and she's looking to pick up a few seasonally people this summer. Just until the Bellagio wedding is over in September."

Normally, Zara would've jumped at the chance, because it was work, and she didn't pass up an opportunity to make connections around the island in case she met someone who could open another door for her.

Anything was better than the door leading to Indian Room.

"I can't," she said, infusing the appropriate amount of disappointment into her voice. "I just picked up that housesitting job I was telling you about. With the show, and now this, I'm not sure I'll have time."

"Oh, that's fine," Ash said. "Hope just said to spread the word. If you know anyone, have them call over to Your Tidal Forever."

"I will."

"So you got the housesitting job?"

"Yes." Zara smiled as she turned onto the road that led back to her apartment. She just needed to pack a few things and get Whitewater, her cat, into her carrier. "I'm pretty excited about it. I'm heading up there right now."

"Pool?" Ash asked.

"*Big* pool," Zara said. "In fact, I think there are two pools at this place."

"I have four dresses to make by next weekend." Ash moaned.

"I'll be here until September," she said. "In fact, I think I'm going to give up my lease." After all, it was only June, and she could save three and a half months of rent if she gave up her place. There were plenty of rentals on the island, and she wouldn't have any problem getting somewhere else come fall.

Not only that, but then the boy band wannabes wouldn't be her neighbors anymore. OH, yes, she was going to give up her apartment, just as soon as she made it back down to town from the bluffs the following morning.

Tonight, she was going to bask in the grandeur of this mansion, maybe sit by the pool, and just *relax*.

––––––––

AN HOUR LATER, THE SUN WAS NOWHERE NEAR SETTING, for which Zara was thankful. She didn't want to pull up to the house in the dark, but Whitewater would not get in her carrier and it had taken Zara an extraordinarily long time to pack a bag and leave her house with the cat. The backs of Zara's hands could testify of that, what with all the scratches from Whitewater's protests.

The cat yowled from the passenger seat, and Zara said, "Oh, be quiet, Whitey. You're fine." So maybe the words held a bit of exasperation. But some of those scratches were deep, and two had bled a little. So the cat could be quiet as Zara navigated the twisty road up to the bluffs.

All of Getaway Bay's rich and famous lived up here. Okay, fine, not all of them. But all the ones who didn't live in the swanky penthouses on the beach. Beachside didn't exist up on the bluffs. Oh, no. People bought these houses for the privacy and security, as well as the stunning, spectacular, three hundred and sixty degree ocean views.

Zara couldn't decide which she'd rather have. Soft, white sand right out her backdoor, or a mansion in the hills. But for the next three months, she'd be taking this twenty-minute drive up to the mansion.

She turned onto the appointed road and went about a block before she met a closed and locked gate. After keying in the code, her excitement grew while the gate rumbled open. A sprawling piece of land sat before her, and she eased her car through the now-open gate onto the driveway.

With the gate moving closed behind her, another sigh passed through her body. She had tomorrow off from swimming practice, as the director was working with the acrobats and the main characters in Fresh Start, the not-to-be-missed show of the summer in Getaway Bay's outdoor theater pool.

Zara had done a few shows at the same venue, and the special effects capabilities were superb. She'd also worked with Ian Granger, the director, several times, and while she'd thought they might have a spark in the beginning, it had fizzled fast.

Just like every other relationship Zara had had. She'd been in the dating pool for a long time, and she was feeling wrinkly and dried out from all the chemicals. She wouldn't care that much that she was boyfriend-less if her mother didn't badger her constantly to find that special someone.

As if Zara hadn't been looking.

She gazed at the beautiful Hawaiian flowers, the trees, the black lava rock in the landscaping. This was done by a professional, and Zara loved every piece of it as she drove slowly past.

The house sat down a little hill and it too spread out and up, boasting tall white pillars on the front porch, which faced the ocean. Of course, three sides of this house faced the ocean, and Zara hoped the room where she'd be staying had a walk-out balcony. Or a patio. Something where she could step from inside to out and breathe in the fresh air and hear the waves crashing on the rocks far below.

She pulled up to the front door and peered through the windshield. "All right, Whitey," she said to the cat. "Let's go see where we're going to be living for a few months."

Petra never had to know about the cat. The woman said she and her family would be overseas for the summer, thus the need for a house sitter. So Zara killed the engine, walked around the car and shouldered her overnight bag before picking up the cat carrier.

At the front door, she keyed in the code and the lock disengaged. The alarm sounded once, and she stepped over to the keypad to disarm it. She hadn't gotten a separate code for it, so she put in the same numbers as she'd used to unlock the front door.

But that only made the alarm beep at her. The steady, every-two-second beeps made her want to stab something in her ears. She tried the code again, very aware of Whitewater's increased yowling. It was as if the cat was trying to harmonize with the incessant beeping.

"Come on," she muttered when she put in the wrong digit and had to go back.

She became aware of another sound amidst the chaos—growling. She turned to see a big, black dog standing about ten feet away, his teeth bared.

"Oh," Zara exhaled most of the word as Whitewater started hissing inside the carrier. The dog barked, huge, booming sounds that filled the two-story high foyer.

With the beeping, and the hissing, and the barking, it was a miracle that Zara heard someone say, "Boomer, be quiet," just before a man came through the doorway and stood behind the dog. He paused when he caught sight of Zara, his eyes widening. He lifted the spatula he held like he'd use it to defend himself if necessary.

"What are you doing here?" he yelled over the barking, the hissing, and the beeping.

"Housesitting," she yelled back. "Who are you?"

He looked like he could be a fashion magazine model, what with that dark hair all swept back into a man-bun on the back of his skull. He opened his mouth, presumably to yell something else, and then rolled his eyes before striding forward.

"I changed the code," he said, practically pushing her aside to punch in the numbers. The beeping stopped. He turned back to the dog. "Boomer, quiet." The dog stopped barking, and Zara tried not to be impressed.

Tried, and failed.

"Sit," the man said next, and the dog did that too.

Now, if she could get Whitewater to stop hissing….

Their eyes met, and dang if Zara didn't have to jump back at the shock she received. He had gorgeous eyes the color of the black lava rock outside, and his olive skin had certainly been featured in many a woman's daydreams about European beaus.

"Who are you again?" she asked, realizing he'd never said.

"I'm Noah Wales," he said. "And I don't need a house sitter."

———

Oooh, Zara's not alone in the mansion! Find out what happens with Zara and Noah in **THE ISLAND HIDEAWAY. You can grab it paperback, ebook, or audiobook!**

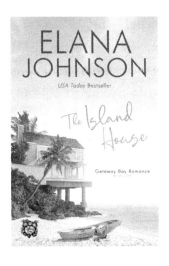

The Island House (Book 1): Charlotte Madsen's whole world came crashing down six months ago with the words, "I met someone else."

Can Charlotte navigate the healing process to find love again?

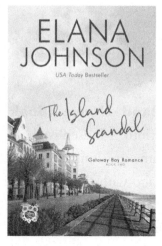

The Island Scandal (Book 2): Ashley Fox has known three things since age twelve: she was an excellent seamstress, what her wedding would look like, and that she'd never leave the island of Getaway Bay. Now, at age 35, she's been right about two of them, at least.

Can Burke and Ash find a way to navigate a romance when they've only ever been friends?

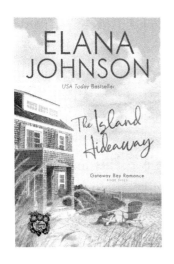

The Island Hideaway (Book 3): She's 37, single (except for the cat), and a synchronized swimmer looking to make some extra cash. Pathetic, right? She thinks so, and she's going to spend this summer housesitting a cliffside hideaway and coming up with a plan to turn her life around.

Can Noah and Zara fight their feelings for each other as easily as they trade jabs? Or will this summer shape up to be the one that provides the romance they've each always wanted?

The Island Retreat (Book 4): Shannon's 35, divorced, and the highlight of her day is getting to the coffee shop before the morning rush. She tells herself that's fine, because she's got two cats and a past filled with emotional abuse. But she might be ready to heal so she can retreat into the arms of a man she's known for years...

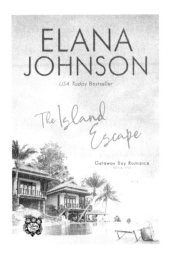

The Island Escape (Book 5): Riley Randall has spent eight years smiling at new brides, being excited for her friends as they find Mr. Right, and dating by a strict set of rules that she never breaks. But she might have to consider bending those rules ever so slightly if she wants an escape from the island...

The Island Storm (Book 6): Lisa is 36, tired of the dating scene in Getaway Bay, and practically the only wedding planner at her company that hasn't found her own happy-ever-after. She's tried dating apps and blind dates...but could the company party put a man she's known for years into the spotlight?

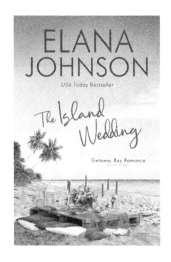

The Island Wedding (Book 7): Deirdre is almost 40, estranged from her teenaged daughter, and determined not to feel sorry for herself. She does the best she can with the cards life has dealt her and she's dreaming of another island wedding...but it certainly can't happen with the widowed Chief of Police.

Books in the Getaway Bay Resort Romance series

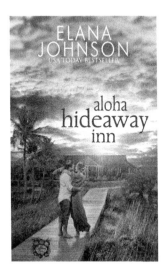

Aloha Hideaway Inn (Book 1): Can Stacey and the Aloha Hideaway Inn survive strange summer weather, the arrival of the new resort, *and* the start of a special relationship?

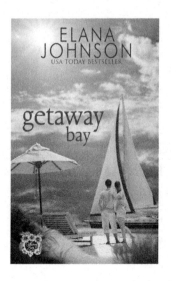

Getaway Bay (Book 2): Can Esther deal with dozens of business tasks, unhappy tourists, *and* the twists and turns in her new relationship?

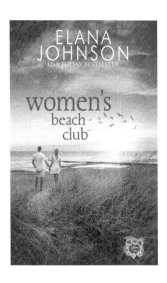

Women's Beach Club (Book 3): With the help of her friends in the Beach Club, can Tawny solve the mystery, stay safe, and keep her man?

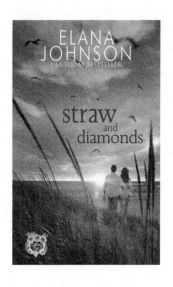

Straw and Diamonds (Book 4): Can Sasha maintain her sanity amidst their busy schedules, her issues with men like Jasper, and her desires to take her business to the next level?

The Billionaire Club (Book 5): Can Lexie keep her business affairs in the shadows while she brings her relationship out of them? Or will she have to confess everything to her new friends...and Jason?

Sweet Breeze Resort (Book 6): Can Gina manage her business across the sea and finish the remodel at Sweet Breeze, all while developing a meaningful relationship with Owen and his sons?

Rainforest Retreat (Book 7): As their paths continue to cross and Lawrence and Maizee spend more and more time together, will he find in her a retreat from all the family pressure? Can Maizee manage her relationship with her boss, or will she once again put her heart—and her job—on the line?

Getaway Bay Singles (Book 8): Can Katie bring him into her life, her daughter's life, and manage her business while he manages the app? Or will everything fall apart for a second time?

Books in the Stranded in Getaway Bay
Romance series

The Perfect Storm (Book 1): A freak storm has her sliding down the mountain...right into the arms of her ex. As Eden and Holden spend time out in the wilds of Hawaii trying to survive, their old flame is rekindled. But with secrets and old feelings in the way, will Holden be able to take all the broken pieces of his life and put them back together in a way that makes sense? Or will he lose his heart and the reputation of his company because of a single landslide?

The Overboard Mistake (Book 2): Friends who ditch her. A pod of killer whales. A limping cruise ship. All reasons Iris finds herself stranded on an deserted island with the handsome Navy SEAL...

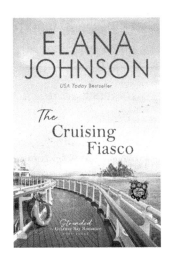

The Cruising Fiasco (Book 3): He can throw a precision pass, but he's dead in the water in matters of the heart...

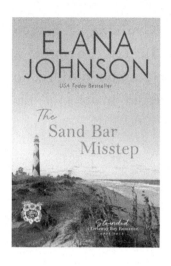

The Sand Bar Misstep (Book 4): Tired of the dating scene, a cowboy billionaire puts up an Internet ad to find a woman to come out to a deserted island with him to see if they can make a love connection...

About Elana

Elana Johnson is the USA Today bestselling and Kindle
All-Star author of dozens of clean and wholesome
contemporary romance novels. She lives in Utah, where
she mothers two fur babies, works with her husband full-
time, and eats a lot of veggies while writing. Find her on
her website at feelgoodfictionbooks.com